A Mer-Murder at the Cove

Related Titles by S. Usher Evans

The Weary Dragon Inn Series
Drinks and Sinkholes
Fiends and Festivals
Secrets and Snowflakes
Beasts and Baking
Magic and Molemen
Veils and Villains

The Lexie Carrigan Chronicles
Spells and Sorcery
Magic and Mayhem
Dawn and Devilry
Illusion and Indemnity

For a full list of titles by S. Usher Evans, visit her website
http://www.susherevans.com/

A Mer-Murder at the Cove

WITCH'S COVE PARANORMAL COZY MYSTERY
BOOK 1

S. USHER EVANS

Sun's Golden Ray
Publishing

PENSACOLA, FL

Version Date: 3/23/24
© 2024 S. Usher Evans
ISBN: 9781945438752

All rights reserved. No portion of this publication may be reproduced, stored in a retrieval system, or transmitted by any means—electronic, mechanical, photocopying, recording, or any other—except for brief quotations in printed reviews, without the prior written permission of the publisher.

Cover Created by Melody Simmons
Line Editing by Danielle Fine, By Definition Editing

Sun's Golden Ray Publishing
Pensacola, FL
www.sgr-pub.com

For ordering information, please visit
www.sgr-pub.com/orders

To RHs3

My forever romance hero
who still wanted to marry me
after renovating The Shack

Chapter One

"Now boarding Flight 612 to Pensacola, Florida..."

There were fifteen people before I reached the boarding agent. Outside the floor-to-ceiling windows, the busy Hartsfield-Jackson International Airport was a captivating scene of planes coming and going. Behind me, a bustling food court and crowded gate area. And in my mind, nothing but dread.

I found my messages app, scrolling until I found the text from an unknown number with a Baldwin County, Alabama area code:

Big Jo died in her sleep last night. Doc thinks it was a heart attack. Memorial service on Wednesday.

I'd responded "thx will be there" as if that were any way to react to the news that the last member of my family had died.

Ten people between me and the gate agent.

I shouldered my bag, carrying my laptop and two days' worth of clothes. My boss at the consulting firm had been nothing but kind, offering his condolences and saying I could work from ("Where is it? Alabama?") as long as I needed. He said it would be like a vacation, going to the Gulf Coast. I gritted my teeth and thanked him for being so understanding.

Five people.

I hadn't been home in eight years, not since the summer my parents died in a late night car crash. I'd taken it as a sign from the Fates that I should follow through on my plan to leave Eldred's Hollow and never look back. And I hadn't, really. Changed my number, ignored most phone calls from my grandmother who dutifully checked in every Sunday, rarely spoke about the tiny little town where I'd grown up.

Three people. Not too late to turn around and go back to my apartment to keep hiding from reality.

Then again, it wasn't *just* that my history was horrifically morose. It was hard to describe Eldred's Hollow without going into some...well, *detail* I wasn't supposed to talk about with regular people. Even mentioning the name was risky, as a Google search would show that it didn't exist.

Two people.

The couple in front of me seemed normal enough, but I caught myself looking for any sign they'd be going to Eldred's Hollow, too. Well, not the Hollow, because nobody ever visited *there*, but the glitzy high rises of Eldred's Beach across the bay. When I'd left eight years ago, the hotels were springing up faster than dandelions along the side of the road. No telling how many were crammed onto the barrier island now.

"Hey there." The gate agent gestured for me to put my phone face-down on the scanner.

I fumbled with it, swiping out of the messages app and searching frantically for the digital wallet—trying to ignore the annoyed sighs of the people behind me. When I found it, I placed my phone down until it dinged then scurried forward down the jetway.

No turning back now. I was going home.

~

The flight from Atlanta to Pensacola was exactly one hour, but the transition from eastern to central time meant I left at 1:02 in the afternoon and arrived at 1:10 local time.

Pensacola International (which is hilarious, considering the only flights are to Atlanta, Miami, Houston, and Dallas) Airport was tiny, and it took me longer to deplane than to get to the rental car counter. I glanced around at the others in line. One couple had what appeared to be makeup smeared over every inch of their face, neck, and hands, and I hid a smile. Found one.

"And where are you going?" the clerk asked.

"Eldred's Beach," the man said, his canines a little more pronounced than a normal human's.

"I'm sorry, where is that?" The clerk gave him a quizzical look, and his wife elbowed him.

"Orange Beach," she said quickly.

The clerk brightened with recognition and gave them directions. Then she handed them the keys, and they went on their way.

I approached the counter with a smile I definitely didn't feel.

"Foley," I said when she asked where I was headed. It was the closest town to the truth. "Funeral."

"Oh, I'm so sorry for your loss," she said. "Was it someone you were close to?"

I'm sure she thought that was an easy question to answer, but it was hard to call Big Jo and I close these days. "My grandmother."

She nodded, as if that were somehow

understandable. I got the usual rental car speech, but I barely listened, hoping it would all be written down in the thick envelope she gave me, and headed out to find my ride.

It was a smart little car, bright red with two doors and not a lot of space.

Big Jo would've loved the color.

Would have. I sank into the front seat and let out a breath. I'd been so focused on getting here, getting my work organized to be without me for a few days, and getting a flight and rental car that I hadn't quite thought about the reason for this impromptu trip. For all the dodging of her phone calls, I did love my grandmother. She was a trip.

Was.

I shook my shoulders and put the key in the ignition.

The drive from the airport to the border between Alabama and Florida was stop and go, full of lights and busy intersections. But once I crossed the Perdido River, the road opened into rolling farmlands and the speed limit increased to 55. The rental was quick, and it was easy to push it far beyond the limit, especially as there wasn't a car ahead of me.

But that meant I got to my destination quicker, and too soon I was turning off the main road onto County Road 95. More farms lined this two-lane road, and I had to pass a tractor that was motoring along at a too-slow pace. At the end of the road sat a large farm of pine trees, along with several alarming signs warning me to slow down, turn around, that there was a dead end. I kept my foot on the gas. While I didn't have a wand on me, the charms would still let me through.

I hoped.

The pine trees came up fast, and I closed my eyes. But my car sailed through, and when I opened my eyes again, the road continued as it had before, with more farmland up ahead of me.

As soon as I was through, I pumped the brakes. Eldred's Hollow Police had very little to do other than writing speeding tickets.

The small town looked...exactly the same as when I'd left. There was the co-op with the cheapest gas in town. Next to it, the wand shop, The Enchanted Cat Cafe that served breakfast and lunch. The bank. A block away, Eldred's Hollow Grocery, run by the werewolves. The post office that did as much snail mail as the magical variety. And the *Eldred's Hollow Caller*, the local newspaper and gossip rag.

I didn't know what I'd expected, but I was at once relieved and disappointed that everything was right where I'd left it. Apparently, the exponential growth in Eldred's Beach was limited to the island. That shouldn't have been a surprise, as it would take divine intervention to change anything here. Fates knew we had enough magic.

I passed the one stoplight in town, grateful I didn't recognize anyone. I was sure I'd see everybody I knew at the funeral, which was set to begin any minute now, but I wanted to get my bearings before I faced the Cove again.

Beyond Eldred's Hollow was more farmland. Witches cultivated the usual soy, cotton, and summer corn. But they also bred livestock that provided wand potion-making material (phoenixes, unicorns, maybe even a small dragon or two) and had ash trees for the wands themselves.

That was what we used to be known for, in fact. Wand making. Until the vampires took over the beach and made it the premier supernatural vacation spot.

Yes, I know. Vampires? At the beach? Believe it or not, the vamps realized there was a market for other supernatural creatures who wanted to enjoy the sun and surf without the regular magical people gawking at them. That, and a clever witch created a balm they could smear on their skin to keep it from burning. Hence the makeup on the couple with the unmistakable teeth at the airport.

But I was daydreaming. Anything to avoid remembering where I was.

Too soon, the green mailbox appeared on the road, and by habit, my foot pressed the brake. I turned onto the dirt driveway, taking in the sight of thirteen acres. The first house on the property was a log cabin with a silver roof and dark windows. From the cobwebs, Big Jo hadn't done anything with it since the night my parents died.

I kept driving, around the pond and over the culvert, until I came to Big Jo's house. She'd built it when my mom and dad had gotten married, saying she didn't want to cramp their style, but she couldn't leave her beloved property. She'd affectionately called it The Shack, and it had absolutely lived up to its name.

It was two stories with one room on each level. The only way to the upstairs bedroom was up a rickety wooden staircase on the outside of the house that probably needed replacing. The whole structure seemed to be leaning to the left, and the weeds around the base were overgrown. It had been painted a vibrant red that had faded, and the front door looked weatherworn and not quite square on its hinges.

I pulled out my key, which I'd never taken off my keychain, and put it in the door. The house groaned as if the wind were pushing it from side to side, and the lock wouldn't turn over.

"Oh, stop it," I snapped at the house. "Don't take that tone with me. Let me in. Just dropping off my things so I can go to the funeral."

The door opened, and I stepped inside, hit with

nostalgia. My grandmother hadn't changed a thing in the twenty-seven years she'd lived here. It still looked like an '80s fever dream, with paneled walls and pink bamboo furniture. A row of cabinets, a rickety stove, and a brown fridge signified the kitchen, and the rest of the space held a couch and some old paintings on the wall. I opened the fridge. It was well-stocked, and the fruits didn't even look like they'd expired. Almost like Big Jo had been expecting company.

The Shack creaked again, and I glared at it. I'd never been sure if it was sentient, magical, or haunted, but it had as much life to it as my grandmother had.

Had.

I slammed the fridge door shut and glanced at my phone. The funeral would get going soon. Not that anything would be on time at the Cove, but it beat sitting here and feeling sorry for myself.

So without a word to the temperamental house, I got back into my car and left.

~

The Cove was a ten-minute drive from my grandmother's house, down a winding road full of interesting houses. There was an intercoastal waterway separating Eldred's Beach from Eldred's Hollow, affectionately called the sound, and the Cove sat on the southernmost point on the Hollow side.

Officially known as Witch's Cove Bar and Marina, my grandmother's place was the quintessential Gulf Coast waterfront dive bar. There weren't any walls, allowing for a panoramic view of the water—though I'd long harbored a suspicion that my grandmother had just been too cheap to add any. An open deck led right down to a white sandy beach. Beyond that was a rickety dock, probably held up by magic, full of different kinds of boats: wooden schooners to speedboats to fishing vessels that brought in fresh shrimp and red snapper from the seas beyond.

The parking lot was covered in white shell gravel, but I couldn't find a spot there. Cars were lined along the road before and after the Cove's entrance, a sign that Big Jo's passing would leave a huge hole in this community.

I drove until almost the very end of the road, well into the residences sitting high above the water, until I found a parking spot. I got out, staring at my reflection in the window. I plastered on a fake smile and pretended I'd seen someone I knew.

"Oh, thanks," I said in a singsong voice. "I know. I'm so sorry she passed."

I sounded ridiculous.

"Little Jo? Is that you?"

I froze, turning to my left where a woman and two small children were walking up from the house where I'd parked. The woman's face sparked something in my memory, and her name came from somewhere in the recesses.

"K-Karen Rose?"

"Karen Shaw now," she said, nodding to the two kids. "Jo Maelstrom. As I live and cast. You're a sight for sore eyes."

"And you've got two kids!" That was the only thing I could focus on. "Wait, Shaw... Did you marry—"

"Ricky?" She shrugged. "Yeah. Not super planned. But you know how it goes. We're making it work."

I forced a smile. Not the most unusual thing to happen in Eldred's Hollow. "That's great. Are you still working at the cafe?"

"Nah, Ricky and I both work at the beach," she said. "He's got a great job as a bartender serving at one of Cal Reaves's hotels, and I sell cleaning potions to the vamps."

"Cleaning potions?" I asked.

She adjusted the baby on her hip and let the toddler run free. "You know those vamps. As much as they like blood, they can't clean it worth a darn. Got my own line of potions now that gets it right out."

Probably explains why they can afford a home on the water. "Are you headed to the memorial?"

"Yeah," she said, her face softening. "I'm so sorry to hear about Big Jo. What a shock. Just didn't wake up one day. How is that even possible?"

"I don't know," I said, and I meant it. I really couldn't understand how an energy like my grandmother's could go out.

She came up beside me. "Come on and walk with me. I'm sure it's about to get started."

The smell of salt water hung heavy on the air, and the soft breeze was cool even as the sun was hot. Karen's two kids dashed up ahead without a care in the world, reminding me that once upon a time, I'd run these streets in the same fashion.

"Third generation of witches growing up at the Cove," she said, as if reading my mind. "Probably going to get them a job working at the marina like we used to do."

"They still do that?" I asked with a laugh. "Suppose not much changes around here."

She grinned at me. "So what have you been up to, Little Jo?"

"Um. It's just…Jo now." I tried to shake off the awkwardness. I hadn't been called "Little" since I'd left. My mom had told me it was the highest honor to be named for my formidable grandmother. When I was four, it was. At thirteen, and chafing under the diminutive moniker, less so. Now it just felt weird.

"Right, sorry. Habit."

"I'm a content management consultant now," I said, answering her question.

"What in the world is that?" She stared at me

like I had two heads. To be fair, even non-magical folk had the same reaction.

"I help organize people's data," I said. "Businesses, mostly. They have all these files and information that's scattered across desktops and hard drives and shared drives. I help them figure out the best system to..." The confused look on her face hadn't dissipated. "It's a non-magical gig."

"Ah, so you still have that issue with magic?"

I tripped over a large shell in the parking lot. *Issue?* That was putting it lightly. "Not really using it too much. Don't need it in my current line of work."

Unsaid was that I didn't even own a wand anymore—not that the one I'd had was any good. It was something of a joke among the Cove kids, Little Jo and her "little" magic. My grandmother swore I'd come into it one day, but despite her best efforts (which at one point included shoving me off the dock and letting the mermaids get me), I hadn't shown much improvement.

And when my parents died, whatever meager magic I possessed dried up like a dead fish on the sand.

Chapter Two

I'd expected a crowd, based on the cars, but there were even more people than I'd anticipated. Mostly witches from around the Hollow, but there were more than a few vampires in the mix. Werewolves, some random demons—I think one might've been a lilin or a nox—and in the water of the marina, a contingent of mermaids. Some had even sprouted legs and stood on the dock, as evidenced by the shiny scales on their legs. There didn't seem to be a happy face in the crowd, and more than a few were wiping tears with handkerchiefs.

I was able to lose Karen as she chased after her kid and was grateful to blend in at the back. Not that I could've gotten any closer, with all the people pressed together. But even from this distance, I could make out the makeshift memorial to my grandmother.

Something twinged in my heart. Her wand. Her pointed white hat (because she lived on the Gulf, why would she need a black hat?). And a rather large Witchwhacker drink.

Witchwhackers were a specialty of the Cove, invented by my grandmother when she'd set up shop in the 1960s. There was ice cream and chocolate in it, plus some type of magical liquor. No one was really sure exactly what went into it except Big Jo. She'd bewitched an old-fashioned slushie machine to never run out of the goods.

I swallowed a lump, hoping that magic held out when Big Jo was no longer there to keep it going.

The murmuring crowd quieted as a middle-aged witch with gray hair came out from the bar area. Her name was Aimee Cheatwood, and she'd been the assistant manager of the Cove since I was a kid. She pulled out a long, thin wand and tapped it to her ankles. She levitated, rising above the sea of heads so she could be seen by everyone.

"Can everyone hear me?" she asked, her voice echoing across the space. "Goodness. What a group, eh? Haven't seen the bar this crowded since our

Fourth of July bash a few years ago when we were giving away that five-hundred-dollar gift card to Cal's hotel. Remember that, Cal?"

My gaze swept to the tall, beautiful man with slicked-back hair. He looked out of place amongst all the t-shirts and cut-off shorts, wearing a pressed white linen suit and shirt. His face was slathered in that same skin-colored makeup, which didn't do much to dispel the look of disgust on his face.

Or was that sadness? Hard to tell with vamps sometimes.

He nodded, his voice dripping with moneyed New Orleans drawl. "It was a magnificent fundraiser."

"Big Jo was…" Aimee's voice cracked and she covered her mouth. "I'm sorry, y'all. I'd told myself I wouldn't cry, but…" Her face screwed up and she lowered back down to earth, sobbing into her hands.

In the crowd, others cried, too, and awkwardness crawled up my spine. Shouldn't I be the one up there, bawling my eyes out instead of gawking like a veritable stranger?

The rational side of me, which had seemingly taken a vacation, returned with a vengeance. I had the overwhelming urge to get in my car, drive back to the airport, and fly to Atlanta as soon as possible.

Unfortunately, my newfound angst drew the attention of the person I least wanted to notice me.

"Little Jo?" Aimee called.

It felt like the entire gathering turned my way, and I wanted to melt into the floor.

"Um. Hi." I gave a little awkward wave. "I—"

"Look at you! All grown up. Your grandmother would've..." Aimee swallowed. "Well, it's not right for me to be up here blabbering on when Big Jo's namesake is standing right here."

My horror grew tenfold. "Oh, I can't—"

But disembodied hands (and maybe a few charms) pushed me forward, through the crowd that parted around me, until I reached the memorial and Aimee, who drew me into a hug before I even knew what was happening.

"Oh, goodness. You don't know how much your grandmother wanted to see you here." She wiped away a tear. "Wouldn't put it past her to fake her own death just to see you."

I froze. "She...didn't, did she?"

"If she did, she put on one hell of an act," Aimee said with a laugh, earning more from the crowd. "But unfortunately, no. She's gone."

I nodded, wishing I felt something more than abject panic. "Well, um..."

"Here, speak up," Aimee said. "Use your..."

I gnashed my teeth together as heat crept up my neck, praying I didn't have to announce it.

"Right." She winced. "Allow me." She gracefully tapped her wand to my throat.

"Ahem." My voice echoed out across the space, and once again, I wished my magic worked well enough to melt me into the floor. "It's uh…nice to be back, I guess. Don't love the circumstances."

A small chuckle rippled over the crowd.

"I know Big Jo would've loved to see y'all here," I said, rubbing the back of my neck. For someone who'd lost everyone in her family, I didn't have a clue what to say at a memorial service. "Thank you for coming."

I turned to Aimee, hoping the wide-eyed pleading would give her the message that I didn't have anything prepared.

"Why don't you tell us a bit about your grandmother?" Aimee said instead.

"Oh, well… You all know Big Jo. Better than me, I guess." Especially in the last few years. "Um… She was an interesting grandmother to have. Never a dull moment, you know? Loved this place. Loved the people, too. Loved Eldred's Hollow." Was I rambling? I felt like I was rambling. "This place was her true love, she used to say. My grandfather was a fling."

Another murmur of laughter, this one a bit stronger.

"Anyway, like I said, I know she'd be happy to have everyone here. Just make sure you tip generously." I looked at Aimee, hoping she wouldn't make me announce that I was done.

Thankfully, this time she took the hint and threw her arm around me. "Little Jo, everybody!"

There was a smattering of applause, and the spell making my voice louder was blessedly released. Aimee then asked the crowd to come up and speak about Big Jo, ceding the floor to a werewolf named Donny before releasing the spell on her own voice.

"I think we need to chat, kiddo," Aimee said, squeezing me to her side. "Why don't we go to the office?"

Besides the bathrooms, the one place that was indoors at Witch's Cove was my grandmother's office. It was a cramped space that smelled of old french fries and had a filing cabinet original to the building.

Ha! Ha! Ha!

I gasped in shock as a white blur flew by my face. I fell backward into the wall, clutching my chest before I realized what it was. A seagull snapped its jaws, giving me a vacant expression as it surveyed me.

"You don't remember Jimbo?" Aimee asked.

"He looks exactly the same," I said with a shake of my head. "Hasn't aged a day."

"Well, you know familiars have long lives," Aimee said as Jimbo began flapping his wings and knocking over papers. "I think Jimbo's been with your grandmother since she bought the place.

Probably eager to get on with you now."

"With me?" I blanched. "I'm not... I don't do magic anymore. No need for a familiar in Atlanta." Let alone Jimbo the Seagull, who I'd always doubted had more than one brain cell.

"Well, you're here, aren't you?" She didn't sound too happy about that. "Why else would you be if you weren't going to take over? The Fates know you never had any love for your grandmother in life."

I opened and closed my mouth. "What's that supposed to mean?"

"It means you broke her heart the day you left, and every Sunday you didn't pick up the phone to take her call."

"I took one or two," I muttered, staring at the disgustingly dirty floor. "On Christmas and her birthday..."

"Lucky her."

"Look, I didn't come here to be interrogated about my life choices," I snapped. "I came to pay my respects, then I'm headed out."

"And what about the bar?"

"I assume she left you in charge," I muttered.

"Well, that remains to be seen, because we haven't found her will yet," Aimee said with more than a little bitterness. "And somehow I doubt she would've given this place to me when she was so eager to have a reason to bring you back."

I swallowed. "I have a life in Atlanta, you know."

"Yes, I hear. Doing all sorts of computer management stuff."

At least she didn't look perplexed by the idea. "I would've come back if I'd known she was sick."

Aimee scoffed. "If she was, nobody knew. They think it was a good ol' fashioned heart attack."

"You'd think there'd be a potion to fix that," I said, pushing a stack of paper from side to side. "I don't think I'm the right person to manage this place. I don't know a thing about it. Be happy to sell it to you."

"You'd have to go through the bank first."

She handed me an envelope with an inordinate amount of red ink on it. I scanned it quickly, recognizing a bank statement and what looked like a mortgage. But that didn't make any sense. Big Jo bought this place decades ago, same as the property down the road. Surely, any debt would've been satisfied by now.

"Why did she take out a second mortgage?" I asked. "And where's the money?"

"I haven't a clue," Aimee said. "I found all this after she passed. Was hoping you could help me figure it all out."

I shook my head. From what this statement said, the money coming in equaled the money going out, and there didn't seem to be much left.

"The bar makes plenty of money," I said. "What

could she need..." My eyes widened when I found the total owed. "Fates alive. Half a million dollars? What did she need that kind of money for?"

She lifted a shoulder. "As I said, your guess is as good as mine. She certainly kept more than a few secrets toward the end."

I couldn't help but notice Aimee wasn't sitting in my grandmother's chair. Like me, she probably didn't feel like she could. We were quite a pair.

"Well, I wanted to let you know first, before the vultures descend." She gave me a brief smile. "As soon as we find that will, we'll sit down with Big Jo's lawyer and figure out the best way forward."

"She had a lawyer?" It didn't seem the kind of person she'd make an appointment with.

Aimee nodded. "Only one in town."

"You'd think he'd set up shop across the water," I said.

"Rent's cheaper."

Couldn't argue with that.

"Surely, he has the will," I said.

"He wasn't involved in that, for whatever reason." She made a face. "He was on retainer for whatever the bar needed."

"Are we sure she had a will drawn up?" I asked.

"He said she told him she did. But he hasn't ever seen it."

I blew air between my lips. Classic Big Jo. Nothing was ever simple with her.

"A lot's changed since you were home," Aimee said. "You should probably get back out there. Folks are eager to catch up."

"Great."

I'd attempted sincerity, but it had come out sarcastic instead. Aimee scoffed again and walked out without another word.

I stood alone in the office. Jimbo's webbed feet stuck to the desk as he surveyed me, though if history was any indication, he was probably looking for food. Eventually, he, too, took flight and headed out into the afternoon.

"Oh, Big Jo. What in the world were you thinking?" I said to the empty space.

~

I took my time returning to the party, and when I did, I headed straight for the bar. It was as rickety as the rest of the place, with metal pieces reclaimed from hurricane debris for an apron, and metal stools that were all taken. For a memorial service, it was lively, with lots of smiles and laughter. Big Jo would've been right at home.

"Well, look what the mermaid dragged in." The bartender put down a plastic cup and poured a bright purple liquid into it. "On the house."

I stared at her for a moment before I recognized her. "Grace?"

She cocked her hip. "Obviously."

Grace was Aimee's daughter and had grown up

with me right here on this sand, though she was a few years younger. Last I'd seen her, she'd had dark hair, freckles, and long limbs that made her tower over everyone else. Now, she was proportional in every way, and her hair was so blonde it was almost white.

"You look…good," I managed. "Great, actually."

"Thanks. I've been experimenting with cosmetic spells. The vamps across the way *love* getting their appearance changed."

"But you're here?" I asked, gesturing to the bar.

"Someone had to serve drinks." Her smile faded. "Doing this as a favor to my mom. She told you what's going on, right?"

I nodded and pulled the drink toward me. "What is this?"

"Oh, hang on." She pulled her wand from between her breasts and tapped the cup. The liquid swirled and turned bright green. "There you go. Midnight Madness is what it's called."

I took a hesitant sip and coughed. I wasn't a stranger to alcohol, but magical liquor was a whole different cauldron.

"Tastes like I'd hate myself tomorrow," I said with a grimace.

"Oh, make a healing elixir and…" She stopped. "Unless your magic is still on the fritz?"

"Thanks for the drink."

I stepped away from the bar and tried to hide.

But the problem with going home was everyone knew who I was. I went from person to person, only a few of whom I recognized, stuck in a social pinball machine to which someone kept adding quarters.

Finally, I managed to get to the open deck, and could breathe a little better. I edged toward the dock, but even that was full of people. Mer-people to be exact. And seeing as most of them lived in the waters beyond the Cove beach, they all knew me, too.

"So sorry to hear about your grandmother."

Maria Greenfin was a few years older than me, with long green hair adorned with seashells and blue scales along her human, bare legs. She sported a pair of cut-off jeans and a white top and held a beer between her hands.

"Nice to see you again, Maria," I said. "And thanks. How are things?"

"Uncle Willard died last year," she said. "So guess who's in charge of the sound mermaid clan now?"

I frowned. "Really? What about your parents?"

"Doesn't work like that," she said. "Duke Pinfish said he wanted to put someone in charge who'd stick around a few decades. So I got the coral."

"How's it going?" I hadn't a clue what being the leader of a clan of mermaids entailed, but I assumed it was like any position of authority.

"The usual," she said with a shrug. "Drunk tourists from the Beach like to throw stuff in the water. I complain to Cal, and he doesn't do a thing about it." She shook her head. "At least your grandmother always tried to keep her side clean. We've never forgotten that she banned that foul mermaid-stunning concoction from boats in her marina. I *hope* it won't be making a reappearance with her demise."

She fixed me with a stare, and I had no choice but to nod. "Yeah, not planning on changing any policies." Especially ones that had nearly caused an all-out war between the mermaids and witches when I was just a kid.

"Just make sure that manager of yours doesn't make any under your nose." She nodded toward the crowd, where Aimee was visible. "She's sneaky."

"Is she?"

"She's always had it in for the mermaids," Maria said with a look. "Never really knew why, but I've had more than a few mermaids say she's scared them off the premises when Big Jo wasn't here. And the mermaids tell me she always carries a vial of stunning potion with her."

"Then I'll be sure to tell her to dump it out." Not that I was planning to be here longer than a few days, at most, but I wanted to get the mermaid's piercing, intense stare off me.

She seemed satisfied. "Good, because things

have changed enough around here."

Another voice came from behind me, and based on Maria's darkening expression, she recognized him even if I didn't. He was our age, with pale skin, dark hair, and a handsome face. If I tried harder, I probably could've found a name for him in my memories, but I was tired of recognizing people—and his focus, for once, wasn't on me.

"I have nothing to say to you," she snapped.

"Then why are you here?" he retorted.

"Paying my respects," she said. "Plenty of deck for the two of us."

I inched backward, sensing that this wasn't a regular confrontation but one with *history*, and their increasingly loud conversation might offer the cover I needed to disappear.

Chapter Three

The next morning, I woke up on Big Jo's couch at The Shack. I stared at the wood-paneled ceiling, remembering the last time I'd woken up here, the summer after my parents died. The couch was still as comfortable as it had been then. Which was to say I was eager to get back to my king-sized bed in Atlanta.

I reached for my phone and unsurprisingly, didn't have a signal. Cell service wasn't too terrible in Eldred's Hollow proper, but out here in the sticks, it was a bit dicey. My work email wouldn't even load, so I searched for available Wi-Fi networks.

Nothing came up.

"Now, I know you told me you have internet here," I muttered to myself, rolling up to sit and rubbing my face.

On one of the few calls I'd taken lately, Big Jo had loudly and proudly announced she'd gotten internet, so now I had no excuse *not* to visit. I glanced around the room for a modem and didn't see anything. I honestly wouldn't have put it past Big Jo to say she'd gotten it to entice me down then scramble to *actually* get it after I made travel plans.

The curtains rustled as if by the wind, and I made a noise. "Good morning to you, too. You didn't hide my clothes again, did you?"

The floorboard under my suitcase moved. The Shack seemed to adore my grandmother, but me? I couldn't tell if it hated me or merely enjoyed my shrieks of horror at its lovely tricks, like moving my underwear to the tree or disappearing the shower curtain and cutting the water as I was ready to rinse my hair.

In the kitchen, the fridge door opened and shut. I quirked a brow. "What do you want?"

The curtains rustled again, and the scent of coffee hit my nose, where a fresh pot was waiting. Gingerly, I stood and inspected it, sniffing the pot.

"It's not poisoned, is it?" I asked as I put the carafe down and searched for a coffee cup in the cabinets.

The Shack seemed to want more gratitude, because it snapped the cabinet doors closed on my fingers.

"Ow! Fine. Thank you." I examined my red fingertips. "What am I going to do with you? You'd probably go insane if you didn't have someone to pester." I didn't know what I was going to do with all of it, to be honest. "Any chance you know where Big Jo put that will?"

A creaking. No answer.

"Didn't think so." I rubbed the back of my head. "Guess I should go see that lawyer today, eh?"

Then I could put this mess behind me and get back to reality.

I drove into town. There were more people out than yesterday, but then again, everyone had been at the memorial. Aimee had given me the lawyer's card, but I didn't need to use my GPS to find it.

With a grimace, I pulled into an empty spot on Main Street in front of the Enchanted Cat Cafe. The number on the lawyer's card matched the decal in front of the cafe, so I assumed he worked in one of the windowed offices above it.

I kept my head down as I tried to figure out how to get upstairs without having to go *inside* the cafe, where half the town would be enjoying coffee, eggs, pancakes, and grits. But there didn't seem to be an entrance, so with a sigh, I opened the door and braced myself for another onslaught.

"Sit anywhere you... Jo?"

The waitress was unmistakable; she looked like she hadn't aged a day in eight years. Kit Meredith had been my childhood best friend, and I shouldn't have been surprised to see her waitressing at her parents' cafe. Being a half-witch, she was something of an anomaly in Eldred's Hollow. I never knew what had caused Kit's witchy mom to fall in love with a green-skinned, grumpy ogre, but at least Kit came out looking human—save some unfortunate knuckle and eyebrow hair she was probably still obsessively waxing off. She, of course, had also inherited the magic that had skipped me, which came in handy as plates levitated behind her.

"Hey," I said with a bashful smile.

"I saw you last night," she said with a knowing look as she walked back to the counter. "Didn't get a chance to say hi before you ran away."

"You know me," I said, awkwardly.

"I do." She sighed. "But it's good to see you. I wasn't sure you'd make it back for the service, but... I gotta say, it made me happy to have you back at the Cove. Even if it was for an awkward speech."

I scoffed. "Aimee accosted me. I was hoping to fly under the radar."

"You? Fat chance." She snorted, putting the carafe back on the warmer. "Hungry? We're serving breakfast for a little longer."

"They've still got you roped into waitressing, huh?" I asked, walking up to the counter.

"My folks are getting up there, you know?" Kit said with a shrug. "Mom doesn't like to stand on her feet as much. Dad—"

"Don't you be telling lies, Kitty," came the gnarled voice of Mr. Meredith from the kitchen. As was common with witches marrying non-witches, he'd taken his wife's name. Two bright yellow eyes set in a gnarled, green face looked back at me from the rectangular window separating the front room from the back.

"Hello Mr. Meredith," I said, waving weakly. For as terrifying as he looked, he'd never been anything but kind to me. Perhaps because, like me, he was a non-magical creature in a sea of wands and hats.

"Good to see you, Jo." He put the plate on the counter. "Order up, Kitty."

"Thanks, Dad," she said, pulling the plate toward her. "Well?"

"Actually, I was looking for a way upstairs," I said. "Need to chat with the resident lawyer."

She nodded to the back. "Stairs that way."

"Thanks." I smiled thinly. "When I'm done, maybe we can have a cup of coffee?"

"I'd like that."

I walked up the stairs, finding two doors at the

top. One was for the Enchanted Cat Cafe's office, and the other said *R. Daniel Page, Esq.*

I knocked and was beckoned inside, where I found a young receptionist popping her gum behind thick-rimmed glasses. A mark on her shoulder told me she was a werewolf.

"Good morning," I said. "I'm, uh…"

"Jo Maelstrom?" came the voice from inside the larger office. "Come on in."

I followed the voice, expecting to see some salt-and-pepper-haired grumpy man seated at a grandiose desk with shelves of legal tomes behind him. Instead, I found a young man, perhaps a few years older than me, sitting behind…well, it wasn't grandiose, but it was a dark wood, and it filled the whole of the cramped space. The air had a faint scent of must, like the dull green carpet hadn't been cleaned in years. It was a stark contrast to the brown-haired, full-bearded man sitting behind it, who didn't *quite* look like a lawyer. He wore a button-up, short-sleeved shirt that probably needed to see an iron, and when he rose to shake my hand, the rips in his blue jeans seemed to coincide suspiciously with the placement of his wallet and keys.

"So sorry for your loss," he said, offering me one of the two seats in front of his desk. "Big Jo will certainly be missed."

"I'm surprised you knew her," I said, sitting

down.

He gave me a confused look. "Why do you say that? I spent every summer at the Cove."

I scrutinized him until a memory jogged somewhere in the back of my mind. My gaze snapped to the law degrees on the wall. "Wait a second…"

His smile widened, and his eyes sparkled with amusement. "Yeah. I used to be much blonder."

That was an understatement. If this R. Daniel Page was actually *Danny* Page, the skinny, tow-headed warlock I was thinking of…the last few years had certainly done wonders. The last time I'd seen him, he'd been all limbs and white hair. Now, his hair was reddish-brown, and he filled his clothes well. I might even call him handsome now.

"How long has it been?" I said, putting my hand to my head, debating if I should ask if he'd taken any appearance-changing potions.

"Well, I think I was a few years ahead of you," he said, sitting back in his chair. "Graduated law school four years ago and set up shop here."

"Why here?" I asked.

"Well, the Merediths are my cousins, you know. And besides that, I love it here," he said. "Went to school in Boston to study the finer points of magical and non-magical law, but I found my calling down here. Especially with all the growth over at Eldred's Beach, I'm busier than I anticipated." He gestured to the assistant outside, who was jamming out to something on her headphones. "Added Mavis last year to answer phones and help me with filing."

I nodded. His time was clearly valuable, so I probably should've called to make an appointment, but he wasn't throwing me out. "So I guess I'm here to ask about Big Jo's will. Aimee said you didn't draw it up, but she had one, right?"

"That's right." He shook his head. "I told her I'd be happy to help, but she insisted she'd had all that sewn up years ago."

"What happens if we don't find the will?" I asked.

He shrugged. "Probably roughly the same as Big Jo wanted. You're next of kin, so everything in her name would automatically fall to you."

I nodded, gritting my teeth.

"Probably not what you wanted, though, right?" He smiled.

"How can you tell?"

"Anyone with eyes could see you didn't want to be there last night," he said with a hearty laugh. "Don't think much has changed since you were a teenager."

I wanted to say a lot had changed, that I'd changed, but I really hadn't. I still felt like the fish out of water, the only person in Eldred's Hollow with a useless wand.

"I have a life in Atlanta," I said, after a moment.

"But I don't want things here to go sideways, you know? I owe that to Big Jo, at least. So what do I need to do to get it into someone else's hands? Like Aimee's?"

He made a face like he wanted to say something, but thought better of it. "Well, I assume the place is free and clear of debts, right? If so—"

"No, it's not," I said with a swift shake of my head. "For some reason, Big Jo took out a half-a-million-dollar mortgage three months ago. The money's been spent, too."

Danny's brows shot up. "What? What for?"

"I don't know. Aimee didn't either. She didn't even know about it until she was digging around in the office after Big Jo died." I paused, not wanting to take the next step, but knowing I needed to. "I should probably figure out where the money went before anything else. Would I be able to ask someone at the bank?"

"You'd have to set up the estate and become the personal representative," he said. "I'd be happy to handle that for you. We'd need the death certificate. Unless you know the passwords to her online accounts?"

I shook my head. "I don't even know if Big Jo had a computer." She certainly *didn't* have internet.

"I've already requested it on my end, but sometimes the family can get it faster. Either way, you're looking at a few weeks," he said, scribbling on a piece of paper. "Unless there was something strange about her death." He paused and looked at me with dark blue eyes. "Was there?"

I honestly hoped not. "As far as I know, no."

He nodded, as if expecting that to be the case. "Once we have the certificate, we can tackle the rest of it."

I pulled out my phone and jotted that down on my notes app. "Okay, so once we do all that, and I've got things figured out... If I wanted to sell the bar to Aimee, how would I go about doing that?"

"If you've got a half-a-million-dollar mortgage on the place, you'll need to satisfy that first," he said. "You're probably better off selling it to someone who can pay full price for it so you can cover the note."

"I don't think Aimee can get a loan that size."

He nodded, and I sensed that might've been what he was going to say earlier. "I don't disagree."

"And as much as I want to wash my hands of everything," I said, "I can't let it go to just anyone, you know? The Cove is an institution. It's made Eldred's Hollow what it is."

He nodded, and I felt a bit like I was trying to convince myself of something.

"Aimee's the best person to take it," I said. "And we'll just have to make that happen somehow."

"I'm sure you'll figure it out."

That must've been lawyer-speak for, "You're

delusional."

"Thanks, Danny," I said, rising.

"Oof, no one's called me that in years," he said. "Well, except my cousin down there."

"Sorry. I hate it when people call me Little Jo, so I'll call you...Dan? Daniel?"

"Daniel is fine," he said. "If I hear anything about the mortgage or the will, I'll give you a call."

"You have my number?" I asked.

He tilted his head and cracked that wry smile. "Who do you think texted you that she died?"

I was comforted by that fact a little. "Thank you for letting me know."

"When are you headed back to Atlanta?" he asked.

"My flight leaves tomorrow, but..." I stood there, realizing that my dreams of popping in and out were most likely a fantasy. Something told me I needed to hang around until everything was figured out, and if the past day was any indication, there was a *lot* to sort through. "Somehow, I wish I'd had the foresight to drive down instead of flying. This rental car isn't cheap."

"I'm sure Big Jo's broom is around there somewhere," he said, sitting back in his chair before wincing. "But you probably don't want to use it."

Considering the last time I'd attempted to ride a broom solo, I'd ended up face-first in the field in front of The Shack, I wasn't in any great hurry to try it again.

"I'll put it on Big Jo's tab."

I walked down the stairs, the weight of the world on my shoulders. Before I continued on into the Enchanted Cat to have that long-overdue talk with Kit, I pulled out my phone and dialed my boss's number.

"Hey, Joel," I said, looking up.

"Jo, how's it going? How was the funeral?"

"Um…" How to explain it? "Fine. But I've hit a bit of a snag."

"What's up?"

"My grandmother's affairs are a bit more complicated than I anticipated. I'd hoped to be back in town tomorrow, but it's looking like I may need to stick around and sort through everything. Is that all right?"

"Of course. Whatever you need. You've got your laptop, right?"

I did, of course—never went anywhere without it. Internet, however, was a different story, but I didn't share that with him. We discussed specifics about clients I was working on and my plan for managing them in my time away from the office. Most of what I did, I could do remotely, which certainly made this impromptu visit down south easier.

"Like I said, sorry to leave you in the lurch, but

I really feel like I need to be here."

"I get it. Good luck. Keep me posted."

I ended the call and sighed, rubbing my forehead.

"He sounds nice." Kit was standing on the other end of the hall, her apron in hand.

"Is it quitting time already?" I asked.

"Not quite, but things slowed considerably," she said. "And not to alarm you, but you've got a visitor."

I blanched. "A *what*?"

"A visitor," she said with a look. "Dad told me to scram, so I'm going to head home and grab a shower. Want to meet me at the Cove for a drink?"

I craned my neck around her, looking for who it might be. "Is there anywhere else we can go?"

"You know as well as anyone there *is* nowhere else in Eldred's Hollow." She walked by and patted me on the shoulder. "See you in an hour?"

"Yeah, see you then."

"And, uh… Good luck with Cal." She made a face. "Try not to sell the place out from under Aimee, will you?"

I did a double-take. "Cal? Cal Reaves? The vampire is waiting for me? What in the world could he—"

She walked out the back door.

Chapter Four

The Enchanted Cat Cafe was empty, save one black-haired man in an expensive black suit facing away from me. I'd never actually had a conversation with Cal Reaves, though I'd seen him around the Cove every so often when he came to speak with my grandmother. I didn't know much about the vampire other than outrageous rumors. He was absolutely filthy rich, from New Orleans, and had cornered the market in hotels across the island.

"Don't stand in the doorway, Josephine. It's rude."

I practically jumped out of my skin, forgetting

that vampires had senses for those sorts of things, then continued walking, trying my best to keep a confident air. Big Jo always said she didn't trust a vampire as far as she could throw them, but she *did* conduct business with them. And Cal had been at her memorial service, which was nice. But perhaps it was politics.

Vamps, as a rule, weren't the gloom and doom that popular media made them out to be. They were immortal, unlike most of the rest of us, and they did subsist on blood. But they considered themselves civilized, and instead of killing random humans, merely set up fake blood banks and took their feedings that way.

However, Cal Reaves was in a class all his own. When I was growing up, he'd arrived on the shores of Eldred's Beach and started snapping up properties. What had once been small, one-story shacks built in the 1960s soon morphed into hurricane-proof high-rise condos and hotels, complete with rooftop infinity pools, indoor gaming centers, and a litany of high-end restaurants. The beach had mostly been inhabited by selkies, who enjoyed a good relationship with the mermaids in the Gulf. I wasn't sure what had happened to them after Cal's bulldozers came through.

Was he planning the same fate for the Cove if he got his sharp canines into it?

"Try not to sell the place out from under Aimee."

My thoughts stopped abruptly when I reached his table. He hadn't aged a single day since I'd first met him as a child, looking more like a twenty-something human than a however-old-he-actually-was vampire. He rose, extending his long, slender fingers to take mine, and I tried not to jump at the coldness of them.

"My *sincere* condolences for the loss of your grandmother," he said, his words dripping like molasses. "But it is *so good* of you to come down and pay your respects. Please, have a seat."

I did so, not entirely sure it was of my own volition. The table was set with a spread of everything on the Enchanted Cat's menu. Syrup pooled atop pancakes stacked ten high, a bowl of cheese grits was steaming next to a plate of scrambled eggs, bacon, and a biscuit. Next to that, a western omelet, BLT, and fried catfish with french fries. It was more than any one person could eat, and I was *pretty* sure vampires didn't eat real food.

Cal seemed to read my mind (or actually read it; my vampire knowledge was a little rusty) and flashed a smile that showed off those pearly white, *sharp* canines of his.

"I hope you don't mind, but I asked Mr. Meredith to whip up some food. I wasn't sure what you liked, so I ordered it all."

I tried not to wince. I'd probably hear all about it from Kit when we caught that drink later. "That's kind of you." Even though I wasn't hungry, I picked up the biscuit and slathered on jelly. "Though I can't imagine you bought all this just to offer your condolences." I gestured toward the grits. "Please."

"Ah, you must not remember much about my kind. Unfortunately, this food isn't nutritious for me," he said, which I took to be code for something else, a look of derision on his face. "But please, eat as much as you like. I'm so sorry for accosting you like this, especially the day after the memorial, but you ran out of the Cove so quickly last night that I didn't have a chance to chat with you."

I picked up the cup of coffee and took a sip, trying to keep my face passive. It wasn't nearly as good as what The Shack had brewed for me that morning, nor anywhere close to the standard I'd get in Atlanta. But it was drinkable, and the food would more than make up for it. After I took a bite of biscuit, I realized I was actually hungry and began chowing down, despite the awkwardness of the one-sided dining experience.

"So." Cal surveyed me over the plates of food. "What are your plans for the Cove?"

Must be that vulture Aimee was warning me about.

I helped myself to the cheese grits, mixing the eggs with them and scooping them onto the biscuit.

"Unclear at the moment," I said, hoping I could keep this vague enough not to give him any hint of what I was actually thinking. "Some things to figure out before I make any decisions."

"Well, let me be the first to—"

"Offer to take it off my hands?" I asked, loading more grits and egg up on the biscuit. "Look, I know you've got a lot of money, but I don't think—"

"I'm willing to offer you two million dollars in cash for the Cove and your grandmother's acreage."

The biscuit stopped halfway to my mouth. "I'm sorry, what?"

"Witch's Cove is *prime* real estate," he said, sitting back and flashing me another wide smile. "The ocean front, the existing clientele. The rich history. I'd be a fool not to add it to my collection."

"I see."

"It's been a few years since you've been back, I hear," he said with a knowing smirk. "I'd love for you to come out to the beach and see what we've put together. I think you'll find that I've kept a careful eye on the past while building the future there. And you can't deny the peacefulness that comes from the Gulf of Mexico."

I doubted that. Eldred's Beach had always been a bit too touristy for my liking. Lots of supernaturals getting a little too drunk on magical liquor and sporting weird tan lines. Besides that, why would I need to travel to the Gulf when I had the perfect oasis at the Cove?

"What are your plans for it?" I asked. "If you

were to buy it from me."

"Does it matter?" He flashed another smile, and my gaze caught on those two pointed teeth again. "You've got a life in...what is it? Atlanta?"

I nodded. "I do."

"And I'm sure you'd be happy to get a nice chunk of change." He sat back, waving his elixir-covered hand. "And the peace of mind of knowing that your grandmother's affairs are settled in one fell swoop. Not to mention that you'd be two million dollars richer."

A million and a half, if that mortgage needed to be paid. But that could go a long way in Atlanta. It was tempting, for sure.

"Just think about it, will you?" He pulled a business card from his pocket and slid it across the full table. "I'm a phone call away."

And with that, he left the booth and walked out the door, leaving me with a half-eaten breakfast sitting uncomfortably in my stomach.

"You'd better not sell your grandmother's bar."

Kit had changed out of her Enchanted Cat t-shirt into a dark purple long-sleeved shirt and jeans. Her long, black hair was swept up into a ponytail, and her eyes were fixed on me the moment I walked into the Cove's covered area.

"Hello to you, too," I said with a look as I took the open seat next to her. "I hope the vamp paid for all that food."

"He's Cal Reaves, of course he did," Kit said. "Dad wants me to swing by after this and clean it all up. Don't suppose you got any magic in the last eight years, did you?"

I shook my head. "I can help, though."

"It'll take you longer than it'll take me," she said as Grace appeared with two beers. "Hope you don't mind, I ordered for you. Didn't think you wanted to tie one on tonight."

"I do not, thank you." The beer, from a craft brewery run by an industrious imp out of Montgomery, was delicious and fruity.

"So you didn't answer my question."

"I didn't." I looked at the bottle. "He offered me two million for the house and the Cove."

Based on the way her perfectly plucked eyebrows disappeared into her hairline, she'd been expecting a much lower number. "Are you gonna take it?"

"I should." I rolled the bottle between my hands. "It'd make this whole mess a lot easier."

"Fates, Jo, you can't possibly be considering it," Kit said, gesturing to the bar around them. "He'll destroy the place. Not to mention your grandmother's property. Are you seriously thinking about selling to him?"

"Calm down. I haven't given him an answer," I said.

"You should have. No."

"Did you know Big Jo racked up half a million dollars in debt?" I asked, looking at her intently.

"What?" She took a sip of her beer. "Why?"

"No clue. Aimee says she doesn't know, either. But the mortgage payment is taking a huge chunk out of profits, to the point where it's hard to keep up with it." I nodded toward the back office, where the door was open. "So something's got to give."

"But the bar? Fates, Jo. Your grandmother would roll over in her grave."

"Good thing she's going in an urn, then."

Kit scowled at me. "That's not funny."

I made a rolling motion. "Easier to roll, you know."

"Jo." She was fighting a laugh. "Not funny."

"Well, when your entire family dies, you tend to develop dark humor," I said, looking out onto the sound.

The ferry from Eldred's Beach, a large white boat with two open levels, was approaching. As the crow flew, the Beach wasn't very far from the Cove, or Eldred's Hollow, even. But to get there, you had to drive all the way north to the interstate, over twenty miles, then take a stoplight-filled road down to cross onto the barrier island. And while broomsticks were useful over land, they were a hazard over open water. So most witches opted for the ferry.

The boat now sidled to the very end of the

marina dock, which seemed to have been expanded in the years since I'd been here last. A trickle of people disembarked, then the ferry kept moving back to the Beach.

"Is Stuart still running things?" I asked, nodding to the boat.

"Oh, yeah. He makes a mint now, what with everyone working at the Beach these days," she said.

"How long has there been a stop at the Cove?" I asked.

"Oh, um..." Kit furrowed her brow. "Maybe five years? Stuart had a dispute with the werewolves who owned the previous dock. You remember where it was, down by the griffon farm?"

I didn't.

"Anyway, of course Big Jo told him he was welcome to use her dock, provided he paid for the expansion."

"That was nice of her," I said. She and Stuart had been friends for as long as I could remember. There'd even been a rumored romance between them, but nothing ever came of it.

"I don't know about nice," Kit said with a laugh. "She's charging him a pretty penny in rent. Not to mention, all the witches and warlocks who work in Eldred's Beach come here to have a drink before going home. I'd say it was a smart business move."

And yet, with all that extra income, Big Jo was

barely making her note. It didn't make any sense.

"I forgot how peaceful it can be here," I said, after a too-long pause. "Not that we ever got peace working the marina."

She let out a snort. Before she'd gotten roped into working at the cafe, Kit had been here at the Cove with me. We'd been in charge of collecting rent from the folks who wanted to park their recreation boats for the day, as well as bringing them food, drinks, supplies, whatever they needed. Of course, we'd often find ourselves in trouble for hanging out on boats with young, strapping tourists and drinking their booze.

"Do you remember that time you tried to get Koby Penfeather onto the Viking boat to make out with him?" she asked, grinning at me.

My face turned bright red. Tried was the operative word there. "Don't remind me."

She laughed. "He's married to Ella Bainbridge now. They took over her father's unicorn farm."

"Man, everyone's married to everyone else," I said, taking a long swig of my still-cool beer. One of the perks of magic. "I saw Karen Shaw—"

"Yeah. That wasn't really a surprise. She and Ricky were always hot and heavy at the high school football games."

"What about you?" I asked. "Anyone catch your eye around these parts?"

She shook her head with a laugh. "If they did,

they'd have to answer to my father, and you know how that would go." She screwed up her face in an uncanny likeness of her father. "Don't you be taking advantage of my little princess!"

"I think Harold Redfin took care of that junior year," I said, giving her a look.

"Sssh!" She looked around with a grin. "What about you? Anyone special in Atlanta?"

"My dating life is as robust as my magical abilities."

She bit her lip. "So...things aren't any better in that department?"

I shook my head. "I don't even have a wand anymore."

"Yeah, I remember when you chucked it into the sound." She cracked a smile. "But surely you've got...something?"

All my life, I'd struggled to conjure, to cast, to do the thing that had come so easily to everyone else in Eldred's Hollow. Both of my parents were gifted magic wielders, and obviously, Big Jo was the most gifted of them all, and always thought I'd come into mine eventually. The night my parents died had been the final straw for me. With all the magic around here, I just didn't see how it could've been possible that a simple car crash could've taken them out. Big Jo had tried to explain it, but I didn't want to hear it. Magic was useless to me, so I'd vowed I'd build a new life without it.

"I'm a wizard at Excel," I said, after a long pause.

She snorted then burst into big, belly-shaking laughter. I couldn't help but join in. It was like nothing had changed between us, and we were a pair of sixteen-year-olds who'd snuck beer from the back room.

We talked for so long that the sun set in the distance and the ferry had permanently docked, but neither one of us had any intention of stopping. The twinkling lights of the hotels across the sound were starting to come on. As much as I'd hated those hotels for ruining my view growing up, they were kind of pretty. The warm breeze off the water, the sound of the waves lapping against the shore, the smell of hot dogs cooking behind me spoke to something in my soul that I couldn't find anywhere else.

"It's really nice to see you," she said. "I've really missed you."

"Me, too." I smiled at her. "Maybe I should make it a habit to come back more often."

"Probably gonna have to if you keep the bar," she said. "May even have to move back."

I stared at my empty beer bottle, turning it over in my hands. Grace had started us on a new type of beer, unasked but not unwelcome. The label had a pretty witch on it, and the brewery seemed to be based out of New Orleans.

"I asked Danny if I could just give it to Aimee, but he said I'd need to satisfy the debt first, and there's no way she could come up with that money. So I probably will have to sell it to someone like Cal." The bar had filled with the end-of-day drinkers. "Nobody'd understand that though. They'd see it as a betrayal."

"If you don't live here, who cares what they think?" she asked.

I did, despite everything. "I haven't made any decisions. First, I need to find an internet connection. I told my job I'd be out of pocket for a few days, but I do have to check in every so often."

"Where are you staying?" she asked. "Eldred's Beach?"

"The Shack." I drank the rest of my beer. "It hasn't hidden any of my clothes or let spiders crawl on me at night, so maybe it's taking a shine to me. Finally."

"Stranger things have surely happened." She chuckled then yawned loudly. "Look, I should probably call it a night. Got to be at the cafe bright and early tomorrow. But I'd love to keep catching up. Will you come by for breakfast in the morning? We have Wi-Fi."

I cracked a smile. "I might do that."

She squeezed my shoulder. "You know, it's really not so bad here at the Hollow."

"For someone who can wield magic," I said.

She opened and closed her mouth then squeezed again. "See you in the morning at the Cafe?"

"Sure thing." I smiled. "Thanks for the chat."

Chapter Five

Kit left me there, and I found myself too enamored by the sound of the water and the warm breeze against my cheeks to move. I'd meant what I said about it being peaceful. Even in the times when I was working, hauling ropes and trays of french fries and hot dogs, there were moments I'd stop and gaze out at the water and remind myself how wonderful it all was.

I tried to envision Cal Reaves owning this place. He'd probably bulldoze it and put a high-rise in its place. The mermaids would flip (hah) and the werewolves, who inhabited the pine forest down the road, would be livid, too. Not to mention that every witch and warlock in the Hollow would have it out for me. Wouldn't be surprised if they hexed me.

But what other choice did I have?

I briefly entertained the idea of putting my consultant hat on and trying to revamp the business. Find more cost savings. Streamline the processes. Trim overhead. But even my imagination wasn't that good. Trying to change this place, which had been run the way Big Jo wanted for over sixty years, was like trying to train the kraken who lived about three miles offshore. The only thing left would be debt and debris.

As I sat there, thinking, Maria Greenfin walked out of the sound, leaving a trail of dripping water behind her. She shook out her long hair and brushed the sides of her cut-off shorts, before the rest of the drying potion she'd presumably imbibed worked.

"Evening," I said, giving her a little wave.

The mermaid jumped. "Oh, Little Jo. I'm surprised to see you still here."

"No one's more surprised than me," I said. "Turns out I can't shake this place that easily."

"I know the feeling." She stared at the shore. "Got some things of my own to work out lately. This leadership business is for the mullet fish." She made a motion like a mullet jumping out of the water.

I whistled. "Oh, man. I haven't had fried mullet in an age."

"I hear the Enchanted Cat is the best place to get it," she said with a knowing smile. "Saw you with Kit earlier. How is she?"

"Same as always. Not much has changed around here, it seems. Except, of course." I turned back to the Cove. "Big Jo."

"Going to be strange not seeing her at the bar," Maria said with a nod. "But with any luck, that'll be the last thing that changes around here for a while."

"What does that mean?" I blinked at her.

"Nothing." She kept walking toward the bar. "I'm going to get a drink."

Aimee was tending bar and gave the mermaid a tense smile as she sidled up. I remembered what Maria had said about Aimee's hatred of her kind, but at least for the moment, all seemed somewhat copacetic. Then again, Aimee was too busy bouncing between the twenty patrons at the bar to spend any time with the mermaid.

Grace had gone home, so guilt prodded me to head back to the bar to help Aimee manage things. I doubted she'd let me, as she'd always been *very* particular, but I'd offer.

As soon as I walked in, I caught eyes with a werewolf my age—the one who'd gotten into an argument with Maria the night before. He didn't seem to notice her tonight as his smirking gaze was squarely on me.

"Well, if it isn't the wandless wonder," he said, glancing at his too-pretty date, who hid a laugh. "Surprised to see you back in town."

His name came back to me in a flash, and my stomach dropped. "Carver Briggs."

Although Eldred's Hollow was full of magical people, there weren't enough kids to fill a whole school, so the young folk attended the local non-magical high school. It made for interesting dynamics, like the werewolf alpha's favorite son swaggering around like he owned every place he walked into. It hadn't helped that he'd been a star on the football *and* soccer teams, which his father encouraged. And even though he didn't have the sort of magic witches had, he could still sniff out weakness and capitalize on it.

"I'd say it's good to see you, but why lie?" I said, after a moment. "What are you doing here at the Cove? Shouldn't you be across the sound at some too-expensive restaurant?"

"As a matter of fact," he said with a look, "we have dinner reservations. But I have business to take care of first."

"Hopefully not with me," I said, praying he wasn't coming to counter Cal Reaves's offer on behalf of his formidable father. I'd been drinking way too much to be able to negotiate fully—not that Big Dog would ever take no for an answer.

"Why in the world would I want to talk to *you*?" He sneered. "You're nobody."

"And you're a little pipsqueak!" said a rough and gnarled voice behind me. Stuart Eaves, the ferry owner, placed a possessive hand on my shoulder. "Get on out of here before Little Jo banishes all the werewolves."

The pup bared his teeth but retreated at the behest of his girlfriend, who whined that they were going to be late for their fancy dinner reservation if they didn't hurry.

"Fine, fine." He turned and scanned the bar before his gaze landed on Maria. "There she is. Damn fish."

Maria popped off the seat the moment she caught eyes with Carver. "'Bout time you showed up, you lazy dog."

"I'm not on *your* time, fish," he shot back.

"Car-*verrr*," the girlfriend whined.

"Go wait in the car, Natasha," he said, waving her off. "I'll be right back."

Surprisingly, his girlfriend didn't argue with him, even though she seemed the type to be jealous of Maria's beautiful face and hair. But perhaps she sensed she had nothing to worry about, as the werewolf and mermaid disappeared into the night glaring daggers at one another. What they had to discuss, I hadn't a clue, but I was *very* grateful I wasn't involved in that particular squabble.

"We're all in trouble if Big Dog decides *he's* the next alpha," Stuart said with a sigh. "Sorry to step in like that, dear. Thought you might need it."

I smiled at Stuart. Like Kit, he was one of the few people I missed here, as he'd been something like a surrogate grandfather growing up. His white hair stuck out from beneath a blue hat sporting the Witch's Cove logo, and his leathery skin was dark from days spent in the Alabama sun. Other than a few new wrinkles, he really hadn't changed much since I'd last seen him, and for that, I was grateful.

"How the heck are you, Stuart?" I said, leaning in to give him a warm hug. "You're looking well."

"Well as can be expected, considering." His dark eyes grew misty, and he pulled a handkerchief out of his pocket to wipe them. "It's a damn shame about your grandmother. She was quite a woman.

"You know Big Jo," I said, gently. "She wouldn't have wanted anyone to make a fuss. Probably how she liked it, going in the night the way she did."

He blew his nose before putting the handkerchief away. "Well, at least it got you back home for a spell, eh?"

"Maybe longer than a spell," I said, an idea coming to mind. "Listen, Stuart, you were one of her closest friends, right?"

He nodded.

"Do you know anything about this half-a-million dollar loan she took out?"

He gave me a sideways glance. "What?" I told him about Aimee finding the bank statements, and he let out a low whistle. "You know, your grandmother had all manner of kooky ideas, but I'm sure whatever the money was going to be used for, she had a good reason for it."

"And that's fine, except that we've got a huge payment on the place now, and the receipts aren't keeping up with the costs," I said. "I just... I can't imagine why she'd put her business in jeopardy like that. It's so unlike her. And then to up and die—"

"You aren't getting into any conspiracy theories, are you?" he asked. "Do you think someone killed your grandmother to get to that money?"

"I don't know, to be honest. Danny Page says he's doing his best to get the information, but who knows how long that'll take? Meanwhile, the place is hemorrhaging cash."

"I wouldn't worry about it," he said. "It's about to be summer, which means all the tourists will be renting boats from across the way and coming here to spend their cash. Whatever money you don't have now, you'll have by September, I'm sure."

The end of summer seemed so far away, and I wasn't sure I could float the bar until then.

"I suppose it doesn't matter," I said with a sigh. "I don't know if it's gotten through the grapevine yet, but Cal Reaves has offered me a lot of money to sell him the Cove and the property down the road."

Disgust flashed in his eyes. "I see."

"I don't know if I should do it," I said, throwing my hand in the air. "It would make things easier, for sure. But...can you imagine Cal Reaves owning this place? What he'd do?" I licked my lips. "You were one of her best friends. What do you think I should do?"

"You're a smart gal. I'm sure you'll make the right call," Stuart said, rising and adjusting his cap. "It was good to see you, Little Jo. Now why don't you run over and help out ol' Aimee before she keels over, too?"

Unsurprisingly, Aimee didn't want my help, but I wasn't quite ready to return to The Shack and call it a night. For one, the beer was still buzzing around my mind, and I wasn't in any shape to drive. I also wanted another look at the paperwork I'd hastily gone through the night before. Perhaps a more thorough look would answer some of the questions swirling in my mind.

With a heavy sigh, I lowered myself into my grandmother's chair and immediately felt like it was protesting the shape of my butt. I adjusted myself, wincing at the loud squeaking noises from the wheels, before finally settling in and turning to the piles of papers on the desk.

I worked for a few hours, only stopping when my eyes crossed. Then I sat back and noticed a small photo above the old 1980s telephone—a faded picture of my parents and me on the Cove beach. Based on our patriotic attire, it must've been the Fourth of July. I was perhaps eight, missing a few teeth as I grinned proudly beside my parents. They held their wands aloft, sparkles streaming out of them.

Something hurt in my chest, a pain I'd done a good job of locking away and ignoring. I pulled the photo down and hid it in the junk drawer to my left.

Ha!

Jimbo swooped in from above, landing on the papers and once again scaring me half to death. The seagull snapped his small, black-tipped beak at nothing and stared at me as if I were a yummy sardine.

"Aren't familiars supposed to communicate with their witches?" I asked, tilting my head.

Ha!

He clipped at the air, and I scanned the room for what he was demanding. Next to my hand, there was an empty basket where a sandwich might've been. Nothing left but a tomato.

"Here, you gremlin."

I tossed the tomato piece to him, and he gobbled it up. It was barely in his belly before he took flight.

"Glad I could be of service," I muttered,

returning to my original task.

The receipts on the desk seemed to be in no particular order, but perhaps that was because we'd already been rifling through them. On top, a receipt for a cooling potion to add to the air conditioner. Beneath that, paycheck data for Aimee and the kids who worked the kitchen in a handwritten ledger. An invoice for the magical liquor and beer. Everything looked as it was supposed to, and there didn't seem to *be* a need for her to take out such a big loan.

"You look busy," Aimee said, coming to stand in the doorway. "Find anything interesting?"

"How did she keep all this straight?" I asked.

Aimee pulled out her wand and tapped it in the air. Before my eyes, all the data that had been on the receipts was magically transcribed onto the ledger.

"That's how," she said. "Quite easy when the magic does the work for you."

My face warmed. "Well, I suppose it would be, wouldn't it?"

"Before you skip town again, I wanted you to have this." She pulled out another wand and placed it on the stack of papers next to me. "Well, Big Jo would've wanted you to have it. I hear you might've lost your other one."

I stared at the worn, wooden stick that had been the instrument Big Jo used to create this whole place. It was so...dull now.

"I don't need it," I said, after a moment, turning

away before I was tempted to pick it up.

"I know you don't *need* it. But maybe you can put it on your shelf or something." She waved her hand. "A witch's wand is her best friend, you know. And I don't think... Big Jo would've wanted you to keep it close."

"Thanks," I said quietly, still not touching it.

She leaned against the doorframe. "Ted Ginny said he saw you speaking with Cal Reaves at the cafe today."

I nodded. "Offered me two million dollars. Cash."

She whistled. "For the Cove?"

"The Cove and the acreage," I said. "Don't know how The Shack would take to having a vampire for an owner."

"Are you...gonna take it?"

I was tired of being asked that question—and even more tired of not having an answer. "No clue. Want to sleep on it a few days before I decide."

She nodded, and it was clear that, in her mind, I'd already sold the place. "Well, I know you'll do what's best."

And with that, she walked out the door.

~

My grandmother's wand was distracting. I kept my distance as if it were a bomb, making sure I didn't trip something. My track record with my own wand was abysmal—I didn't want to think what I might do with one this powerful. Or maybe it was a conduit, and my grandmother's skill was what had made it such a formidable weapon. In my hands, it might be a good paperweight.

As if proving a point, I picked up the wooden handle and held it aloft. There wasn't so much as a glimmer of magic. No tingles up my arm, no brisk wind that told me *this is it!* Just a boring stick in my hands.

I wasn't sure what I was expecting, but the nothing that happened disappointed me. Perhaps some part of me had hoped my grandmother's death would be the thing that propelled me into my full abilities, and taking up her wand... It was stupid. Even thinking about it made me cringe.

I wafted it around, as I'd seen her do a million times, feeling nothing magical coming from my body. I may as well have been an orchestral conductor.

"Horns," I muttered, gesturing to a fake orchestra pit. "And in with the violins now. Come on. Louder!"

I chuckled as I inspected the wand, no longer afraid I was going to set the place on fire. Witches' wands were made by taking a piece of wood, usually ash, but Big Jo had chosen a pine tree from her property. The wood was then left to soak in a potion unique to each wand, which allowed it to conduct magic from the witch's body. Witches often compared wand potion ingredients when introducing themselves, but I couldn't remember what Big Jo's potion had entailed. Perhaps I should've asked her.

I put it out in front of me, holding it between my forefinger and thumb as I'd seen her do a million times.

"Find Big Jo's will," I said, lifting the wand.

And to my surprise (and horror), something tingled down my arm, like a long-lost memory of a skill, twirling from my fingertips and surrounding the wand,

The world went dark.

I wasn't unconscious because there was a cool breeze on my skin. The smell of the sound. The waves. I was on the beach somewhere.

But based on how dark it was, I wasn't anywhere near the Cove itself.

"Great. Just great." I stuffed the wand into my back pocket. "This is why I don't do—"

I tripped over something and fell face-first onto the beach. I spat out a mouthful of sand and rubbed in vain at my hands and cheeks as I looked around for what I'd stumbled on.

My heart sank into my stomach when I found myself looking into the dead eyes of Maria Greenfin.

CHAPTER SIX

I didn't quite remember how I'd called for help, but there was more than a little screaming involved as I ran down the beach. Somehow, I'd found my way to the Cove, and Aimee had deciphered my hysterics enough to alert the police. Within moments, five magical policemen appeared, and I had the unfortunate task of returning to Maria's body. One of the cops cast a bright light into the sky above us, illuminating the beach in grotesque detail. I turned away, unable to stomach the sight of someone who'd been *alive* not an hour ago suddenly dead.

"You'll be all right," Aimee said, rubbing my shoulders in a motherly sort of way. "Poor Maria."

I nodded, grateful she was there to keep me steady. We both stared at the body, unable to speak, holding our breaths while the police did their inspections. Some part of my brain told me I should turn around and go home, but I knew the moment I did, I'd be seeing her dead eyes looking back at me.

"You're the one who found her, Jo?"

Vinnie McDaniel was another Cove kid, a bit closer to Danny's age than mine. It seemed he'd followed in his mother's footsteps and joined the Eldred's Hollow police force. For all my jokes about how they only wrote speeding tickets, they seemed to be on the ball, as they weren't fazed by the dead body like I was.

"Jo?" he prompted again. "You were the one who found her, right?"

Numbly, I nodded.

"If you're feeling up to it, I have to ask you a few questions," he said, giving me a once-over. "Why don't you start at the beginning?"

Yikes, how far back should I go? "I was…taking a walk on the beach," I said, deciding against going on the record about how I was using my grandmother's wand and cast the wrong spell. "It was dark, and I could barely see. Tripped over her. Called for help." I shuddered. "What do you think happened?"

He closed his pad, which had been magically writing everything I said. "Unclear. Kind of looks like she suffocated."

"Suffocated?" I put my hands to my throat and swallowed. "What makes you say that?"

"Well, she still had her tail, and she was found on land."

"Her…" I hadn't even noticed a tail. Too focused on the pair of dead eyes staring back at me.

"Goodness," Aimee whispered.

"It seems she was doused with mermaid-stunning potion," he said, giving Aimee a too-long stare. "But we'll have to run some tests to know for sure."

"I can't believe she's… I saw her tonight, at the Cove," I murmured, more to myself than to him. "She was…well, she was alive, then."

His pen began scratching on the pad behind him. "What else can you tell me?"

"She left with Carver Briggs," I said, my heart sinking into my stomach. Carver was a pain in the butt, a ridiculous spoiled brat, but…a murderer? Even as much as I disliked him, it was hard to reconcile that idea. "They didn't seem happy about it, either."

"Leaving together?" He looked confused. "Maria was leaving with Carver?"

"He said something about unfinished business or business or something like that," I said, scratching the bottom of my brain to remember the details. "Told the other girl to wait in the car. Then he came out onto the beach with Maria." I shook my head. "But he's not a murderer. He's an ass, but..."

He let out a loud sigh. "You'd be surprised what people are capable of. Regardless, he's already on my list."

"Really?" I frowned. "Why?"

"That's right, you haven't been here in a while," Vinnie said, rubbing the back of his head awkwardly.

"Carver and Maria were involved. Really involved," Aimee said.

There wasn't anything really dramatic about a werewolf and mermaid dating. "And?"

"Well, it was volatile. Always getting into some big argument in the middle of the Cove," Aimee continued, when Vinnie didn't say anything. "Then the next day, together like nothing was wrong. Carver thought he was the more impressive of the duo, of course. But when Maria got her big promotion, she dropped him like a bad habit. And I'm sure you can understand how Carver took that."

I doubted the man had ever experienced rejection before that. "Maturely, I'd guess."

Vinnie snorted. "We've been called out here a number of times because of their arguments. Thought it might've lessened when he got his new girlfriend a few weeks ago, but..." He looked back at Maria's body. "Perhaps not."

"He spoke to her the night of Big Jo's funeral, too," I said, my memory finally coming back to me in full force. "They seemed to be arguing then, as well. Can't tell you what about, but..."

"Probably the same thing they've been arguing about since they broke up," Aimee said.

"I wish I could remember more," I said, a little more eager to help than was necessary. The more I thought about it, the more I liked the idea of Carver Briggs spending a night in jail. I doubted it would humble him any, but it would sure give me great pleasure.

"And you said you were just...taking a walk?" Vinnie asked. "In the dark?"

"That's me," I said with a laugh I hoped didn't sound nervous. "Town weirdo."

Aimee watched me carefully, as if she knew I was lying, but blessedly, didn't say anything.

Vinnie didn't look like he was buying it, either. "Well, if you think of anything else, give me a call."

He handed me a basic business card with the Eldred's Hollow Police Department logo and his contact info—most prominently, a wand call sign. I was grateful a phone number was right underneath. I didn't plan on using Big Jo's wand again any time soon.

I stuck his business card next to Danny's in my

pocket. Had it really only been one day since I'd arrived? It seemed like so much longer.

"Come on," Aimee said. "Let's get you back to the Cove."

We walked the short distance back, not a word said between us. I plopped down at one of the picnic tables near the water and put my head in my hands while Aimee went to get something to steel my nerves. I wasn't eager to drink more alcohol, but perhaps I needed it. The bright light of the police's spell was close, attracting the attention of everyone at the Cove who stood around discussing the scene with beers in their hands. I was grateful none of them came over to question me, because I wasn't sure I'd be nice if they did.

Suddenly, my whole world went white. I blinked, rubbing my eyes to clear them. Then another flash blinded me.

"Jo Maelstrom, as I live and breathe!"

I recognized that voice and groaned loudly. "Lewis Springer. If you don't get that camera out of my face, I'm going to smash it."

The photographer backed away as my eyes readjusted to the darkness. He was tall and gangly, as he'd been as a teenager, but he'd grown out his hair into a large afro and was now sporting what appeared to be an attempt at facial hair. He wore a wide, eager smile and there was a pen hastily scribbling on a notepad behind him. But unlike

Vinnie, there would be nothing "official" about Lewis's report.

"Just wanted to see if you'd give a quote to the Holl-Call," he said, inching closer to me. "It'll be the front page tomorrow. Second death in town in one week. Probably a record."

I'd purposefully avoided reading the local newspaper because most of the stories were egregiously made up. That, and I'd never forgiven Lewis's uncle for somehow getting photos of my parents' car crash and plastering them on the front page for a week straight.

"Here's a quote," I said, rising to leave. "Beat it."

"Back in town, eh?" He scurried around to block my path. "How long are you planning on staying? Are you going to be selling the bar? Word on the beach is—"

"Word on the beach is that if you don't get out of my way, I'm going to throw you in the sound and let the mermaids deal with you."

"Oh, is that any way to treat a fellow Cove kid?" He flashed another smile.

I glared at him as I moved to walk away. "Yes."

He blanched then scampered to stand in front of me again, the camera following behind him. "Look, just a quote. You were the one who found her, right? What did Vinnie say about it?"

"Ask Vinnie."

He was undeterred. "What were you doing out

on the beach when you found her?"

"Sunbathing, obviously."

"Is there any truth to the rumor that she was arguing with Carver Briggs the night she died?"

I opened my mouth, and the brief hesitation was enough to confirm it for him.

"Yes! I knew I saw them talking." He inched closer. I hadn't even seen the weasel at the bar, but I hadn't been paying that close attention. "What did they say? Was it a passionate lover's quarrel? Did it get physical? Spare no detail—"

I sighed, looking up at the moon and gauging whether I wanted to try hexing this annoying cub reporter with Big Jo's wand. But then again, I might end up in Paris if I attempted it.

Paris did seem nicer than here, though.

"All right, all right, take it easy," he said, watching me reach for the wand. Apparently, he was the only one in town who'd forgotten that me and magic didn't mix. "Just trying to get the truth."

"So is Vinnie," I snapped. "And he won't add a bunch of speculation to his truth, either."

He brushed off my words. "There's a lot going on in town you might not know about. This isn't just any mermaid—"

"I'm aware of who she is," I drawled, closing my fingers around the wand.

"Then you'll know that you want me on your side," he said. "The mermaids are going to blame you for this."

I whirled on him, fire in my veins. "I'm sorry, what? Me? What did I have to do with anything?"

"Oh, Duke Pinfish is going to have a *field* day. Or...whatever mermaids have." He cackled, almost gleeful. "You know, he's never liked the Cove or the witches speeding up and down *his* waterway. Now his favorite clan leader shows up dead on your beach? You'll be lucky if he doesn't flood the place."

"Lewis Springer, if you don't get off Cove property in the next five seconds, I'm going to hex your face green." Aimee stood on the deck, glaring at the reporter, who wilted under her attention. She held a mug of something steaming in one hand and her wand in the other, pointed at him.

"A *thousand* apologies, Ms. Aimee," he said, backing up. "Just trying to do my civic duty and—"

"Five, four, three…"

He yelped, conjured his broomstick, and took to the sky before she could finish counting. It was so dark that he disappeared quickly, but I still waited a good few minutes before exhaling in relief.

"Here." Aimee handed me the mug, which, when inhaled, loosened more of the tension in my skull. "You look like you needed a pick-me-up, and you've clearly had enough beer tonight."

"Thank you," I said, taking a sip. The taste of lavender hit my tongue, and the rest of the nerves melted from my body. A calming draught. I hadn't had one since...well, since *that* night. But in my relaxed haze, I couldn't even dredge up the memory. With a sound that wasn't entirely human, I sank back down onto the picnic table and let the steam hit my face.

"Glad I could be of assistance," Aimee said with a chuckle.

"This is incredible," I said, more drunk than I'd been with the beer. "You're incredible. Thank you. I take back all the mean things I said."

She made a face. "What mean things?"

I honestly couldn't remember. "I'm sure I said something mean recently."

"It's been a weird week," she said, her gaze landing on the bright lights in the distance. "First Big Jo, now Maria? I can't remember the last murder we had in Eldred's Hollow. No wonder Lewis was so excited." She clicked her tongue. "He's got all the unfortunate qualities of his uncle and none of the shame."

"Thank you for dealing with him," I said. "No telling what would've happened if I'd tried hexing him." I felt her piercing gaze on me. "What?"

"You told Vinnie you were walking on the beach," she said slowly. "But I'd left you in the office five minutes before you started screaming."

The relaxation evaporated. "And?"

"And unless you managed to sneak out of the office without me seeing, which is impossible, and speed walk to the other end of the beach, which is also impossible..." She tilted her head. "What really happened?"

I cleared my throat, glad the dark night hid my burning cheeks. "Well, I might've...attempted a spell with Big Jo's wand, and it went a bit sideways."

"Attempted?" She chuckled. "What did you try?"

"I asked the wand to find Big Jo's will," I squeaked.

"You..." She seemed to suppress a laugh. "Okay. And what happened when you did that?"

"I ended up at a murder scene," I finished. "Should've known using someone else's wand was a recipe for disaster. Using my own wand usually was, too."

There was something like pity on Aimee's face. "Do you still have it?"

I nodded, reaching into the back of my pants to pull it from my waistband. I didn't remember sticking it in there in my mad dash back to the Cove, but I clearly had.

"Well, at least you didn't chuck it into the sound this time," she said softly.

I nodded, placing it on the table between us as if it were a poisonous snake. "Probably won't be using it anymore, though. I've had my fill of surprise trips lately."

She snorted as she sat beside me. "I can't believe

Maria's dead. She was so young. Just a few years older than Gracie. She had a life ahead of her, too. Can't imagine who would want to hurt her."

Aimee looked shell-shocked, and I couldn't help my curiosity. "Maria thought you didn't like her that much."

"I mean, I don't like mermaids in *general*, but I didn't mind Maria. She, at least, had spent enough time on land to know that we all gotta coexist. The other mermaids, especially ones over in the Gulf, seem to think they own everything. They can kill, hurt, and ruin lives, and get away with it because they've got some deal with the bigwigs in New Orleans."

"What do you mean?" I asked. I had only a cursory understanding of the supernatural law enforcement system, having rarely interacted with anything beyond Eldred's Hollow.

"Duke Pinfish, the lord of the Gulf, he's on some council in New Orleans with the rest of the supernaturals. I hear they've got a couple witches, a vamp—maybe even Cal Reaves, for all I know. A werewolf, I'm sure. Maybe some more creatures I don't even know about." She paused. "And they decide what punishment gets doled out for these things. And typically, if a mermaid is involved, there *is* no punishment."

"You seem to have some experience in this arena," I said softly.

She nodded, her eyes growing distant. "Gracie's father was a warlock who fished in the Gulf. A mermaid decided that he'd taken one too many fish and toppled his boat. He never came home." She sighed. "We'd separated by then, but it still wasn't fair. Nobody was arrested. Nobody held accountable. Just because one day a mermaid got a funny idea."

"Surely the other members of the council have some sway," I said.

"They told me the mermaids were going to have their own justice," she said with a scowl. "But I never knew if they actually went through with their promise, or if they thought his death was justified." She sighed. "Maria wouldn't have been involved in that, and she seemed a fair leader during the few weeks she was in power. But I can't help the way I feel about the rest of them. Especially Duke Pinfish."

"You don't think he's going to cause trouble for us, do you?" I asked, thinking back to what Lewis had said. "Obviously, Maria's death wasn't our fault. It was probably Carver Briggs."

"Carver?" She snorted. "He's a pup. All bark and no bite."

"Yeah, well, he sure was *barking* a lot at Maria this evening," I replied.

"It's as I said, they bark all the time," Aimee said. "Look, I'm going to close up for the night.

Why don't you head on back to The Shack and get some rest? Maybe tomorrow, we'll both wake up and realize this has all been a horrible dream."

Chapter Seven

"*Fates alive!*" I screamed as I opened my eyes the next morning.

Something warm and wet was on my face. I swatted, and the object flew to the ground. As my vision cleared, and my brain reset, I realized it was a piece of buttered toast.

The Shack curtains rustled, as if offended I could *possibly* have been startled by such a thoughtful gift.

I rubbed butter off my face, still unsure if this was The Shack being nice or mean or something in between. But there *was* coffee in the kitchen, so I could absolutely forgive the sentient house for the rude wakeup. It wasn't as if I'd slept well anyway.

My dreams had been plagued with visions of Maria's body, of her arguing with Carver Briggs, and, grotesquely, what it must've been like for a mermaid to die on land like that. Not wanting to dwell on *any* of that, I chugged a cup as fast as it would go down my throat and stared at the pond beyond The Shack.

A scaly blue head popped up and stared back for a moment before unfurling a long, slender tongue to snatch a dragonfly zooming by. Then it disappeared back into the water.

"Well, that's new," I said, pouring the rest of the coffee from the carafe into my mug.

I turned to face the living room and tapped my fingers against the warm mug. My laptop sat open on the floor, but without internet, it was as good as dead. I probably needed to get to the Enchanted Cat to connect, but instead I turned my attention to the papers I'd brought home from the Cove last night. When I couldn't sleep, I'd started going through them in more detail until exhaustion finally took hold.

I sat cross-legged on the floor, placing my coffee mug next to me and picking up where I'd left off. This morning, these papers made as much sense to me as they had the night before. The mortgage had been taken out three months ago, and the money withdrawn to an unknown account via wire transfer three days later. I'd been able to find statements of her personal checking and savings account, and the money wasn't found in there. It was just…gone.

Complicating matters further, if my math was correct, the money coming into the Cove was roughly equal to the money going out. This last month, there hadn't been more than five dollars left at the end of each month. Even with (I assumed) magic to keep the lights, air conditioning, and water pump on, there was still a running tab with Eldred's Hollow Grocery for the meat, magical liquor that she ordered from the distributor out of New Orleans, and the general maintenance that came with the marina.

I sifted through the papers four or five times, until I finally gave in and accepted I wasn't getting the answers I needed. I hadn't even gotten around to submitting the request for the death certificate, so I turned to my computer to tackle that first before remembering why it was turned off in the first place.

"Okay, we'll tackle *that* first," I muttered, pushing myself to stand.

Although I was *very* sure Big Jo had been lying to me about getting internet, I still wanted to give the old bird the benefit of the doubt, so I scoured the small downstairs for a modem or router. Nothing.

I stepped outside, gazing up at the telephone

pole next to The Shack and the wire that led to the house. Lights and pumps could be run by magic because they were self-contained. But things like telephones and internet needed to connect to the larger world, hence the pole. I *did* know my aged grandmother had a landline because that was how she'd called me every Sunday.

The wire from the pole to the house seemed to be for the telephone, but that might work. I doubted there were fiber optic cables running through the farmlands of Alabama, so DSL would probably be my only option. At least I wouldn't have to call someone about running a line down the property.

In the meantime, a biscuit at the Enchanted Cat didn't sound so bad.

I dressed quickly and got in the car, throwing my laptop into the passenger seat. As I drove up the dirt road, my gaze wandered to the bright red berries that dotted the brambles around the pond—blackberries. Big Jo would make all kinds of sweets from the blackberries we'd pick, from using the leaves in potions to blackberry cobblers and jam. But they were delicious even off the vine, the juice warm from the sun.

Beyond the pond, there was the log cabin, where I'd grown up. The day my parents died, Big Jo had locked the front door and told me to come stay with her. I hadn't set foot in it since, and I had a sinking suspicion Big Jo hadn't, either. If I opened the door now, using the key that was *also* still on my ring, I'd almost certainly find everything exactly as it had been.

I shivered. Not a theory I wanted to test.

No, those ghosts were better left buried. And the log cabin could stay…well, locked up and unused, if that was how Big Jo had left it. I had enough problems without adding more to my plate, and reopening wounds from my childhood didn't sound like a good idea.

What did sound like a good idea was working through the checklist Daniel had given me so I could get back to the real world.

The Enchanted Cat Cafe was busier than the day before—and somehow looked bigger, too. No… *was* bigger. Yesterday, there had been three tables in the center and six booths. Today, I counted no fewer than twenty tables and ten booths, all filled with happy customers drinking coffee and inhaling everything from cheese grits to pancakes to hash browns.

Kit was breezing from table to table with a huge grin on her face, with plates coming and going from the kitchen by magic, sometimes trailing her, sometimes floating on their own accord. But as soon as I walked in the front door, all conversation and activity stopped as every gaze landed on me.

I realized, a little too late, that by now, every witch, warlock, demon, vampire, and werewolf probably knew what had happened at the Cove. And I was, perhaps, the topic of conversation on everyone's lips.

"Morning, Jo," Kit said, breaking the uncomfortable silence. "Breakfast?"

"Please," I said, my voice coming out strange. "Need to do some work."

"Bar's open." She nodded toward the front of the room. The bar was not, in fact, open, until she pointed her wand at it. The wall rearranged itself, and the bar stretched until it was large enough to accommodate another setting, complete with a stool popping up out of the ground.

"Thanks," I said, clearing my throat as I walked through the center of the room, feeling the gazes and curiosity of everyone there. Thankfully, it was a short walk, and I was careful not to catch anyone's eye. Once I reached the chair, I quickly opened my laptop and began typing, hoping and praying the conversations would start up again.

I opened my laptop, but before I could even look at connecting, I felt a stare on the back of my neck. When I glanced around, Bobby Cutter, a warlock who owned one of the fishing boats in the marina, was glaring at me with a toothpick between his teeth. Ironically, he was also wearing a Witch's Cove hat, but his love for my grandmother didn't seem to extend to me.

"Can I help you?" I asked, spinning around in the chair and crossing my arms over my chest.

"Yeah, I gotta bone to pick with you. Now that you're the owner of the marina."

"I'm not..." But I supposed I was. At least for the moment. "Yes, Bobby, what is it?"

"I need you to do something about these infernal mermaids. Your grandma was too soft on them. Letting them get away with wrecking boats and causing trouble."

"Strange thing to say, considering their leader died on the beach last night," I said, quirking my brow.

"Good." He sniffed. "That Pinfish fellow's too strict with the fishing quotas. Used to be we could go out and catch what we could. Now, I gotta have a darn chart to keep straight what fish we can catch and when."

I failed to see how any of this was my problem, but I'd dealt with clients long enough to know how to placate irate idiots. "What would you like me to do?"

"Talk to who's in charge down there now and tell 'em the next time they put a hole in my boat, they'll end up like Greenfin."

"I wouldn't be saying that too loudly," Kit said, walking by and placing a plate of pancakes in front of him. "Considering we don't know exactly what happened to her."

"Murder, obviously." A shrill-voiced woman with perfectly curled hair put down the paper she was reading—and based on her expression, I knew which one it was. "Someone had it in for Maria Greenfin. We have to figure out who it was."

"Well, you know she and Carver were on the outs again," said an older man beside her. The mark on his shoulder said he was a werewolf, but I didn't recognize him.

"And Carver has *quite* the attitude," the snooty-faced woman replied.

"Don't go blaming werewolves for this, Dottie," Kit said, pouring more coffee into her cup. "For all we know, it was another mermaid who did it."

Dottie, clearly a witch based on the wand by her left hand, picked up the coffee and sipped it. "I'm sure they'll do what they do best and bury the truth under the sea."

A murmur of agreement rippled through the crowd. Clearly, the truce my grandmother had created between the mermaids and witches wasn't quite as settled as I'd thought.

"Ignore them," Kit said, casting them a nasty glare. "They're starved for interesting conversation." She paused in front of me and leaned over the counter. "Seriously, though. Are you all right? I heard you were the one who found her."

I nodded, taking another long swig of coffee.

"Eat that, please," Kit said, pointing to the untouched breakfast. "You can't subsist on coffee alone."

I scowled and took a bite of toast. "Yes, mother."

The front door opened again, and Daniel walked in wearing a short-sleeved, button-up plaid shirt, slacks, and boater shoes that had seen better days. For a lawyer, he certainly didn't dress the part—maybe a benefit of working for himself.

Kit pointed her wand, and the bar once again extended, adding another stool. He thanked her as he put down his messenger bag beside me. Almost immediately, a plate of eggs, bacon, cheese grits, toast, and a stack of pancakes appeared in front of him, along with a sweet tea.

"Thanks, Kit," he said, grabbing the tea and taking a swig.

"No coffee?" I asked, eyeing his plate. "Also, that might be the fastest service I've ever seen."

"Don't be too impressed," Kit said, walking around the front of the counter to refill my coffee. "Danny comes in every morning at exactly ten o'clock and gets exactly the same thing. Dad has it ready for him."

Daniel flashed her a grateful smile and dug into the food.

I returned to my laptop and finally logged in, going to connect to the internet. There were several Wi-Fis available, and none of them seemed to originate in the cafe.

"That one," Daniel said, pointing to the corner of my screen. "Password is password, lower case."

"Thanks," I said, typing it in. "And thanks for your excellent timing. Thought Bobby Cutter was gonna deck me before you got here."

He frowned and looked behind him to where the fisherman was glowering into his pancakes. "Why?"

"Apparently, he wants me to do something about the mermaids," I said, looking at the notes app in my phone to start working on the checklist.

"Search for the Alabama Bureau of Vital Statistics," he said, sipping his sweet tea.

"What?" I turned to him.

He pointed to my laptop with his glass. "Alabama Bureau of Vital Statistics."

I did as instructed, and when the website came up, he directed me to click, click, click, click until I reached the form to fill out the request.

"Glad I ran into you," I said after a moment. "Though it does seem rather strange to be using the regular Alabama state resources. Doesn't Eldred's Hollow have anything like that?"

He shook his head. "There's a big gray area where the magical world and regular one collide. Lots of things the magical folk didn't want to have to create a new system for, lots of things we need to get the job done. Especially in my line of work. I'm having to navigate both sides of the courts."

"Must be fun," I said, filling out the form with my driver's license and other information.

"I'm not bored, that's for sure," he said.

"What do you do, mostly?" I asked.

"I call it door law," he said. "Basically, anything that walks in the door. Property law, family, estates on occasion."

"Any criminal law?" I asked as a figure in blue landed on his broom outside. Vinnie. Something told me he wasn't here for the grits.

"Not specifically," he said. "Do you need a lawyer for that?"

"I hope not," I said as Vinnie walked through the door. I used the non-existent magic in my veins to will him to go to anyone else, but his gaze landed on me.

"What's going on?" I asked.

"The tests show she was doused with mermaid-stunning potion. We need to search Witch's Cove for evidence. Thought you'd like to be there when we did."

"O-of course," I said, after a moment.

No one in the diner looked surprised, so they'd obviously all heard the scuttlebutt about her cause of death. I, however, thought it incredibly odd that he was giving me a heads-up and asking me to come with him.

But when he beckoned me to follow him and

stood in front of his broomstick with a sidecar for a second person, I held up my hands. "I'm not getting on that thing."

"It's a broomstick," he deadpanned.

"I don't ride broomsticks," I said with an equal amount of deadpan. "Remember?" I pulled the keys to my rental out of my pocket. "I'll follow in a good ol' fashioned car, thank you."

"I'm coming with you," Daniel said, walking out with his briefcase in hand. "And I got your tab."

I'd completely forgotten about that. Not that Kit would mind if I dropped by later to pay it. "Thanks."

"Well, hurry up. We're not waiting for you," Vinnie said, hopping onto his broom and taking off.

"Why do you think he came to me first?" I asked Daniel.

"Probably best if we do what he says," Daniel said, opening the passenger door to my car and getting in with his briefcase. "Let's go."

"Don't you have a broom?" I asked, getting in beside him.

"I do," he said with a nod. "But if I used it, we wouldn't be able to talk."

"We need to talk? About what?" I turned on the engine. "Are you my lawyer now?"

He smirked. "Was I ever not?"

"I mean, not officially," I said. "And I'm not sure I can afford your hourly rate…"

"Let's call this a pro bono consultation until we know what you're up against," he said. "Especially since I have a feeling Vinnie has a suspect in mind. There's no other reason he'd have come to you first. Probably doing you a favor to make sure someone's there."

"I mean, Aimee's there. I..." I paused, my eyes widening. "You don't think Vinnie's going to arrest *her*, do you?"

"They found mermaid-stunning potion on Maria," he said. "Aimee's rumored to carry it. If they find it on her, they'll have enough cause to arrest her."

He looked worried. Aimee was curt and brusque, but she wasn't a killer.

Was she?

CHAPTER EIGHT

The drive from the cafe to the Cove was short, and Daniel didn't ask me any more questions. In some weird way, I was glad he was there. I wasn't a damsel in distress, by any means, but things were moving into a gray area out of my depth.

I ran through the last few conversations I'd had with Aimee and Maria over and over again. Aimee had seemed sad about Maria's death—spooked almost. But was she spooked because she'd caused it?

Maria had said there was no love lost between them, and Aimee had confirmed it by saying Grace's father had been killed by mermaids. But she'd also told me she had no quarrel with Maria. Was that the truth or was she just trying to cover her tracks?

I was *really* starting to wish I'd picked up the phone when Big Jo had called. Maybe I'd have some insight into the personalities I'd left behind—and a bit more clarity on who amongst the witches, warlocks, and other supernatural creatures might be capable of murder.

As Vinnie had said, the Cove was already swarming with magical law enforcement. Two werewolves were on their hands and knees—in human form, no less—sniffing the beach. Several others were questioning the boat owners (including Billy Cutter, who'd flown here faster than I could drive). I didn't see Aimee anywhere, which made me nervous.

"Any words of advice, o wise lawyer?" I asked as Daniel stepped out of the car.

"Don't say anything," he said, his face darkening as he followed me onto the deck.

Raised voices drew us to the bar, and I found Aimee, red-faced and furious, in a shouting match with Vinnie, who looked smug and held a pair of handcuffs.

"What's going on?" I asked.

"Good, Little Jo's here," Aimee said. "Tell this impertinent little—"

"Aimee..." Daniel said warningly.

"*Tell him* that you were with me before the mermaid died," she said.

I glanced at my supposed lawyer, and he nodded briefly. "I told you, Vinnie. Aimee and I were in the office."

"And you also said you left her there and went out for a walk," he said. "Then came across the mermaid."

"So what? You think she beat me to the mermaid and left her on the beach so I could find her?" I scoffed. "I mean, I know Aimee's mad about me taking over the Cove, but—"

"You're mad about it?" Vinnie said, and in my periphery, Daniel rolled his eyes.

"What she means is—" Daniel began.

"*Thank you*," Vinnie said. "No one's under oath, so we don't need a lawyer here."

"Can we all take a step back?" I said, holding up my hands. "Why Aimee? I told you that I saw Maria and Carver arguing. Why not bother him?"

"Carver has an alibi," Vinnie said.

I clicked my tongue. "Does he have an alibi or did Big Dog tell you to back off?"

"Jo," Daniel warned, but I glared at him.

This smelled too much of the Eldred's Hollow powers-that-be meddling. Big Dog Briggs ran Eldred's Hollow Grocery, but he'd made sure members of his pack had infiltrated everything in town, from the bank to the co-op to the small police force. And I was quite sure every one of those werewolves answered to the alpha, not to justice.

"Everyone in Eldred's Hollow knows Aimee hates the mermaids," Vinnie said. "I've got accounts from five witnesses saying that last week, Aimee was hounding them off the property."

"They were drunk," Aimee said with a glare. "And using their magic to harass the non-water folk."

"The way I hear it, the merfolk were trying to prevent a Cove marina boat from dumping their trash into the water," Vinnie said. "And you took the witch's side."

"Again," Aimee said through gritted teeth, "they were drunk. Billy Cutter was ornery and threatened to hex them. I told them all to go home. Pretty standard around here. Go talk to him about it if you want."

"Do you have any sort of evidence to charge Aimee?" Daniel asked.

"I do, as a matter of fact." Vinnie tapped his wand to the air, revealing a small vial suspended in a clear bubble-like spell. "We found this empty vial of mermaid-stunning potion in the office with Aimee's magical fingerprints on it."

I couldn't tell a mermaid-stunning potion from hair dye, but based on his smirk on his face, I guessed that was the murder weapon.

"That's not mine," Aimee said, reaching into her

pocket. The vial she held was identical to the one Vinnie had, but there was still a purple liquid in it. "I've carried the same potion in my pocket for the past fifteen years. Never used it once."

Vinnie quirked a brow. It wasn't quite the slam dunk she was hoping for, in my eyes, and based on Daniel's expression, he didn't think so either.

"Besides that, you still don't have motive," Daniel said, after a too-long pause.

I flashed him a brief smile, grateful he'd come along with me.

"How's this for motive?" Vinnie said with a sneer. "Last night, Aimee got into an argument with Maria, who'd come to discuss the new regime after Big Jo's death. The argument turned physical. Aimee, in self-defense, doused her with a vial of mermaid-stunning potion. We all know she carries it around with her since her ex-husband's death."

Aimee gritted her teeth, and Daniel stepped forward.

"Vinnie, you know this is all speculation," he said.

"Except the mermaids have given sworn testimony that Maria was going to discuss the future of the Cove with someone last night," he said. "When she didn't return, they came looking for her and found the police around her dead body. Now, who else would she be discussing the future of the Cove with if not Aimee?"

"Me?" I folded my arms across my chest.

"Are you sure you want to be volunteering yourself? You're the one who found the body," Vinnie said with a look.

I cleared my throat. "What motive would *I* have? I literally got here two days ago. But what I do know is Aimee was with me moments before I found Maria's body."

"And how is that possible if you were taking a walk?" Vinnie asked.

It was my turn to blush, feeling like an idiot. But if I wanted Vinnie to leave Aimee alone, I needed to come out with the whole truth, as embarrassing as it was. "Because I wasn't taking a walk. I…uh…" Fates alive, this was like nails on a chalkboard. "I tried to use Big Jo's wand."

Vinnie let out a low snort, and even Daniel looked at me sideways.

"I…" The words came with difficulty. "I was trying to find her will after the conversation I'd had with Aimee. Thought it might be faster if I summoned it to me."

"Hasn't it been several years since—" Daniel began.

"*Yes, it has*," I snapped, my face turning even more red. "Look, I'm trying to get back home, so I was doing whatever I could to find the thing. Instead, it transported me to the beach where I found Maria's body." I tightened my arms across my chest, hating the way everyone stared at me like I was some kind of freak.

"Are you seriously trying to tell me you used transportation magic?" Vinnie said with a quirked brow. "There aren't but a handful of witches and warlocks in town with that kind of magical ability, and you want me to believe that you…uh…you could do it by accident?"

"Believe me or not, but that's the truth," I said, wishing I could melt into the ground.

"You have to admit, it's a bit too implausible to be a lie," Daniel said.

I didn't know whether to thank or slap him.

"As it stands, we still have enough evidence to charge her," Vinnie said, pulling out his wand. "Aimee Cheatwood, you're under arrest for the death of Maria Greenfin."

I opened my mouth to argue, but Daniel quickly shook his head, and I closed it. Aimee allowed herself to be magically handcuffed and led out of the bar to where two officers had a broom between them. They placed her on it, linking their brooms to hers, and lifted into the sky, floating toward town. Vinnie then turned on his heel and went to talk with three of his officers.

Daniel and I stood in the Cove, neither of us speaking for a long time. He was the first to break the silence. "I suppose I'd better get down to the station with her."

He pulled out his wand and lowered it slowly, a stylish mahogany broomstick appearing. Once it was fully formed, Daniel snatched it out of the air and headed toward the deck of the Cove.

"Wait!" I called, walking after him.

He turned with a quirked brow.

"Thanks," I said. "I think she's innocent, by the way. The timing just doesn't make sense."

"I know she is. That's why I'm going to help her," he said with a half-smile. "You stay here and keep the bar running. I know you need the money."

With that, he hopped onto his broom and took off, leaving me alone inside the Cove bar. It felt strange, the whirring of the Witchwhacker machines, the magic humming in the air, keeping the beer cold. I chewed my lip and looked around, unsure what to do next.

Vinnie was over by the dock, speaking with a merman who seemed much larger than any I'd seen before. He had a broad, russet-colored chest partially covered by a thick smattering of white hair, and a long beard. He carried a large spear, and the water that held him aloft swirled around a purple tail. On his head was a coral crown.

Was that Duke Pinfish?

With gaze narrowed, I left the shade of the Cove and walked toward the dock where Vinnie seemed to be wrapping up his conversation with the merman. If I wanted to speak with him, I'd have to hurry, as I wasn't going to be jumping into the sound to swim after him.

"Duke Pinfish?" I said, rushing up to the two of them.

The merman turned to me, his dark brown eyes scanning me while he scowled.

"I'm Jo Mael—"

"I know who you are."

I swallowed a catty retort. "My condolences for the loss of Maria. She was…" I didn't think I should lie. "I'd heard great things about her new role."

"And I have your despicable bar employees to thank for it," he said, turning to me. "Should've sunk every boat in this marina and flooded the place years ago. Nothing but a cesspool of alcohol and debauchery for careless supernaturals."

"Nice to meet you, too," I muttered.

Vinnie scoffed and rolled his eyes. "I'll be in touch, Duke Pinfish."

He walked away, and I got the sense the mermaid was about to leave, too. "Aimee had nothing to do with this," I said, hurriedly. "She was with me."

"And I should trust you because?"

"Because I have no reason to lie to you," I said.

"Your kind lie all the time. Your grandmother promised me *and* Maria that all instances of that horrific potion would be banned from your shores. And yet your own second-in-command was known to carry it. How is any mermaid supposed to trust one of your kind anymore?"

"You're clearly trusting the police," I said, gesturing to Vinnie's retreating back.

"They're a means to an end. I sit on the council in New Orleans for all magical creatures in this area. I will be ensuring that justice for Maria is accomplished quickly and will be taking the culprit to our underwater jail."

I frowned. "That's not... Can she breathe underwater?"

"We aren't barbarians," he said with a sneer. "She will be uncomfortable, but not dead. But that's a fitting punishment for the way she treated Maria."

"How are you so sure it was Aimee? I heard Maria arguing with Carver Briggs the other day. Why don't you go harass Big Dog and see if his son had anything to do with it? It's always the boyfriend, you know."

"Maria very smartly broke off their relationship weeks ago, and they were quite amicable."

That wasn't what I'd seen. "Look, don't assume you have the murderer because it's the most obvious, easiest solution. Whoever killed Maria might still be out there, plotting another mermaid's death. We should be focused on *that*, not on innocent people."

Pinfish gave me a once-over. "If you've got such a problem with your own police, why don't you investigate yourself?"

I didn't have a response to that. It wasn't my job to get in the middle of this any more than I already had by finding her body. But there seemed to be a strong current of opinion going against Aimee, and if I didn't stand up for her, who would?

"Maybe I will," I said, lifting my chin. "I hear Maria was set to meet with someone the night she died. Something about the future of the Cove. Any idea who that was?"

"The person I thought it might've been has been arrested." He moved to leave before stopping to look at me over his shoulder. "I've given the word to all my mermaids that they're no longer allowed to frequent your bar," he said. "Clearly, it's a hazard to our health."

"That's not—" Mermaids made up at least a third of the Cove's revenue. Not the best time to be losing money. "You can't do that."

"Can't I?" He chuckled. "I'm the leader of all the mermaids from Cozumel to Miami and beyond. I can *do* whatever I want." The vortex of water brought him closer, until I could practically count the water droplets on his toned chest. "And if you aren't careful, you might find yourself on my *bad* side, Miss Maelstrom. I don't think you'd like to see what happens when the mermaids decide you and your witchkind are no longer allowed to use our waters for your *recreations*."

I swallowed, but didn't retort as he dove back into the water. I stood there for a long time, waiting for the waters to calm, before walking off the dock to where Vinnie was waiting.

"You'd better watch that silver tongue of yours, Little Jo," he said. "Lot more at stake around here if you tick off the mermaids."

"And you'd better do your job," I said. "Aimee is innocent. Just because you've got King Triton over here pressuring you for a culprit doesn't mean you can pick the first person whose fingerprints you find and call it a day."

He scowled, and that was all the confirmation I needed that he was phoning this in. But before I could press him further, he left me on the dock.

I spent two hours rage-cleaning Big Jo's office before my blood pressure finally came down. Jimbo flew in to watch me, but when he realized he wasn't getting any food, he disappeared. Some familiar he was.

I found more bank statements, though none that answered the burning questions of the day. Plus some very old fry basket paper, a copy of the Holl-Call from 1993, and an invoice from Eldred's Hollow Grocery from three years ago.

After I came down from my anger, I sank into Big Jo's chair, wishing that it somehow smelled like her still. One week, and the whole place had gone to pot. Aimee arrested. The mermaids refusing to come to shore to spend their money. The place barely making ends meet. And here I was, sitting in her chair like I had the right to manage any of it.

I stared at my phone, wondering if Daniel would pick up and give me an update. Surely, some level-headed judge would look at the evidence and let her go. And then Vinnie and the police would be able to focus on finding the real killer.

Something about Maria's death seemed very personal, as if someone had wanted to take revenge against her and her alone. There were, of course, plenty of people who might want a mermaid in power dead. Another mermaid could've been the one to do it, if they hadn't had such a visceral hatred of the stunning potion (for good reason). Someone like Billy, who'd always run afoul of the mermaids in his business, could've grown tired of her and wanted her out of the picture.

Then, of course, there was Carver. A man used to getting what he wanted would certainly have motive to kill his ex, especially if she'd been the one to dump him. Carver wouldn't take rejection lightly, especially if he was in the running to take over from Big Dog.

Not to mention…

Cal Reaves, the very man I'd been about to implicate in my thoughts, sat at the bar.

Chapter Nine

"Good afternoon, Jo," Cal said, that thick southern accent like nails on a chalkboard. Today he wore a white linen suit that seemed a little too nice for the slum he stood in. "I'm so glad I caught you."

"Are you now?" I hadn't a clue why a vampire might want a mermaid dead, but if it was Cal, it probably had something to do with business. I'm sure I wasn't the only one he was trying to buy from, though I didn't know what Maria might've had to offer him. "Unfortunately, we aren't open yet. Been a bit of a crazy day."

"So I hear. Just positively *awful* what they're

saying about Aimee." His words slid over his tongue like molasses. "I don't for a minute believe she was capable of what they're saying. Murder?" He tutted, as if the creature didn't subsist on human blood. "In this town? It's an absolute travesty."

His protests were starting to sound a little like guilt to me. "She's innocent."

"Of course she is," Cal said with a look that was borderline patronizing. "Can't imagine she'd have a quarrel with sweet Maria Greenfin. The mermaid was such a bright light in this community. And what a nasty way to go, too. Someone was clearly angry with her."

"Have any thoughts on who it might've been?"

"I can't say I do," he said. "You know I like to keep my ear to the ground, and I've never heard a single person say a bad word about Maria. I half expect it to be a case of the wrong place at the wrong time, you know? Maybe some fisherman uncorked the wrong bottle. These things happen."

"Big Jo outlawed that stuff on this beach," I said mildly.

"And yet, Aimee carried it around."

"So everyone says," I said. "Which is odd, because Big Jo always made such a fuss about the agreement. Why give Aimee a pass?"

"I can't presume to know what was in your grandmother's heart," he said, patting his own chest. Did vampires have hearts? "But she always had a soft spot for Aimee. Let her get away with all sorts of things." He sighed. "But I'm sure you know all that."

"Mmm." I kind of did, but I wanted him to keep talking.

"Well, I know you're busy," he said, rising slowly. "I just wanted to stop in and ask if you'd given any more thought to my offer."

"Been rather preoccupied," I said, picking up a rag from behind the bar and wiping down the wood. It wasn't dirty, but I wanted to keep my hands busy so he wouldn't see my annoyance.

"There seems to be quite the mortgage on this place," he said, looking around.

I stopped scrubbing and looked at him. "How do you know that?"

"One hears things when they're a pillar of the community, like I am," he said. "Quite the mystery, what your grandmother took it out for." He twirled a straw between his fingers. "I do have a theory, though."

"Yeah? What's that?"

"Well, you aren't the first person I brought this offer to," he said. "I'd obviously asked your grandmother if she'd consider selling. It was clear keeping this up by herself was taking its toll on her, and perhaps I was right. Her poor heart just gave out, after all." He tutted. My suspicion grew. "Maybe she took out the mortgage to give herself an advance on the money she'd be getting from me."

"Why would she do that?"

"Your guess is as good as mine," he said. "But the fact of the matter is that you've got this debt, and *now* the leader of the mermaids has banned a good portion of your patrons from spending their money here."

My lips pressed into a thin line. "And how do you know *that*?" It hadn't been more than three hours since Pinfish made his decree. Either news traveled fast underwater, or Big Dog wasn't the only supernatural who had informants on the Hollow police force.

"We've suddenly had a surge of mermaid customers on the other side of the sound," he said with a shrug. "Word gets around."

It sounded plausible, but I wasn't sure I believed it. "Mm."

"If I were you, Jo, I'd want to be rid of this place," he said, running his finger along the wood as if I hadn't cleaned it. "I'd give you cash. Can take over the place in a preliminary fashion until all the paperwork clears. Quick, painless, and you're back to Atlanta and your old life, a million and a half dollars richer. Doesn't that sound lovely?" Another fanged smile.

"It does sound lovely," I said, even though the thought of selling to Cal made me feel gross. "But I'd be remiss if I didn't keep a steady hand on things during this transition period. Daniel says it'll take a few weeks to sort it all out."

"Ah, young lawyer Page?" He chuckled. "Bright young man. Well-educated. I've sought him out a few times myself."

I *highly* doubted a vampire as rich as Cal Reaves had used Daniel's services. He probably had some slick lawyer who cost a thousand dollars an hour.

"My answer right now is no," I said. "But I'll be sure to let you know if that changes."

He nodded and swept from the bar toward his very expensive foreign car like a shadow. I took a little pride in the fact that the ground-up shells in the parking lot left a white sheen on his tires and bumper, though I was sure there was a waiting witch or demon or whatever vamps hired to keep their stuff clean.

I put down the rag and noted the time. The bar would really get hopping in a couple hours, and I hadn't even showered. I'd planned to after knocking out the checklist Danny had given me, but I was pretty sure the death certificate form was still half-finished on my computer.

Had it only been a few hours since I'd walked into the Enchanted Cat?

"Ugh." I rubbed my face. I couldn't leave the Cove without anyone here to watch it. There were coverings that came down to close the place at night, but without magic, they were as good as useless to me. I could lock the office, but I didn't have a key to get back in.

I stared at my phone. If I hurried, I could get home, shower and change, and be back before the afternoon rush. And I wasn't completely alone.

I went to the kitchen to retrieve a frozen french fry and held it up. A *ha ha ha* echoed from somewhere, and Jimbo swooped down to try to snap it from my fingers.

"Uh-uh," I said, pulling it away from him. "Listen up, birdbrain. I'm headed back to Big Jo's for a shower. I will be back within the hour. Don't let anyone steal booze or money, got it?"

He clapped his beak, but I wasn't sure if that was in agreement or if he was trying to get the french fry.

"I'm trusting you, because Big Jo wouldn't have kept you around if you weren't useful in some way." I tossed the potato at him and he swallowed it in a single gulp.

Then the little turd flew away.

"I'm trusting you," I repeated after his retreating back. Without any other options, I hopped in the car and sped back toward The Shack.

Of course, nothing was ever as easy as it seemed. When I arrived back, the front door wasn't there. The steps now led up to a solid red wall..

"Very funny," I said, tilting my head up. "I need

to get back to the Cove. Can you please let me in?"

The only opening in the wall, a window, cracked open.

"Do you think I can reach that?" I said, hopping off the stairs and walking toward the window.

It was at least two feet higher than my head, and even when I jumped, I could barely get my fingers on the sill. As soon as they made purchase, they slipped off, and I landed in the sticker bushes I would've sworn hadn't been there when I'd walked over.

"Could you *please* let me inside?"

It creaked and groaned as if it were laughing at me.

"*Fine.*" I marched to the back deck, pulled myself up, and tried the sliding glass door there. No such luck. I briefly considered chucking one of the wooden rocking chairs that sat to my right at the glass, but knowing The Shack, it would probably chuck it right back.

I glanced up. Maybe if I could at least grab a fresh shirt…

Big Jo's room was upstairs, and until now, I hadn't been able to bring myself to go up there. I wasn't scared or anything, but it felt like a breach of privacy. Even though she was gone, even though this place was probably mine (so Daniel would say), it wasn't mine. It was, and always would be, hers.

The stairs leading to the second floor were old

and rotten, and it was with *much* trepidation that I tested the first step. But to my surprise, it held my weight without as much as a creak. More enchantments, perhaps, or The Shack itself doing its best to keep the stairway's integrity.

I climbed, huffing at the stupid house and its stupid games. A hotel might actually be less stressful at this point. Except that I didn't really want to spend the money on one. Not to mention, the only hotels nearby were owned by Cal Reaves, and I didn't want to chance him showing up at my door and pestering me about selling.

The stairs ended in a balcony and another sliding glass door, leading to the bedroom. To my utter surprise, the door moved when I pulled on it. Inside, Big Jo's room was cramped, with a sloped, wood-paneled ceiling that came right down to the floors. To one side, a closet had been cut out and a single bar hung inside with a suite of t-shirts and jeans. In the center of the room was a queen bed, stripped, with two bedside tables. Everything seemed a bit too neat and clean for what I remembered of my grandmother, which made me feel all the more awkward standing there.

My gaze fell on a photo on the bedside table, and it drew me closer.

It was me and my parents on the day of my high school graduation. Less than a week later, they'd be gone, and I'd become a shadow of this grinning teenager. But in this photo, we looked ecstatic, like the world was our oyster. I could hear them talking to me, congratulating me on the honors and accolades I'd received (even if they weren't magical ones), the sound of my mother crying, the loud boom of my father's voice. It was as if this photo had been enchanted to replay the moment over and over again.

Not for the first time, I wondered how my life would've turned out if they hadn't taken that ride. Would my magic have finally matured into something usable? Would I have been like Kit and Karen, staying in Eldred's Hollow instead of striking out on my own?

No. Leaving had always been my path, no matter what. I'd felt constricted by the small town and the people in it. Hadn't loved that everyone knew my name and my history. I'd wanted a fresh start in a new place—and I'd gotten it.

But as much as I'd fought to leave this place, being back here didn't feel as suffocating as I'd always feared.

I put the photo down and turned back to the closet, grabbing one of the Witch's Cove t-shirts from the rack and carrying it downstairs. When I reached the last step, the downstairs sliding glass door was open for me, and from the sounds of it, the shower was on.

"Temperamental little..." I muttered, glaring at

the building as I marched inside.

Freshly showered, and with Big Jo's shirt on and her wand stuck under the back clip of my bra, I returned to the Cove to find a few cars in the parking lot. I internally winced—who wanted a drink at four o'clock in the afternoon? Then I remembered it was Friday, and this place was a vacation town.

Silly me.

I ran but almost immediately skidded to a halt. Aimee was behind the bar, pouring drinks and laughing as if there wasn't a problem in the world. Jimbo was perched on the Witchwhacker machine, eyeing a plate of fries.

Aimee spotted me, and her expression darkened significantly.

"You're...back?" I said, walking up to the bar. "What in the world—"

"I made bond, obviously," she said. "And good thing I did. The bar was completely unattended."

I forced a smile. "I was gone maybe forty-five minutes."

"And there were people waiting half an hour," she said, nodding at a pair of suntanned men who were drinking beers. "Luckily, Sam and Ted are regulars and can help themselves. You didn't even *lock the place up*."

I bit my tongue instead of responding the way I

wanted to. "I'm glad you're back. Do you need me to hang around, or…?"

"Stay out of the way. Or better yet, go home."

"You're out on bond," I said, pointedly, as she breezed by me. "There's a not-small chance you could be in jail at the bottom of the sea soon. Maybe I should hang out here and learn how to sling drinks."

"I've got it covered," she said. "Go home."

"I'm sure you do, but if they find you guilty—"

"They won't."

"Did you hear that Pinfish told the mermaids they weren't allowed to come here anymore?" I asked, following her into the back storage area. I was quite sure she could've summoned the objects she needed, but she was trying to get away from me.

"I did."

"And?"

"And we'll figure it out."

"Why are you being such a…" I swallowed the word I wanted to say. "I'm here to help, Aimee. I'm not trying to change anything—"

"Then why were you talking with Cal Reaves?" She spun around to glare at me.

"He showed up to ask me to sell him the bar again," I replied evenly.

"And?"

"I told him no." I gestured toward the marina. "Not until we figure out what the heck is going on here. And not until we find that half a million dollars."

"Say you find it. Then what?"

"One step at a time," I said, after a moment. "And I'm here. Teach me what you know so I can keep this place going if the worst should happen."

She sighed, turning to me fully. Her gaze fell to my shirt. "Did you steal that out of your grandmother's closet?"

I thumbed the hem. "Yeah. The Shack wouldn't let me inside until I took it."

Aimee snorted. "You know, Big Jo never did quite figure out what she did to that place to make it so ornery. She thought for a while she might've awoken a ghost, or maybe it was the combination of spells she used to ensure that her needs were taken care of. But good to know it's keeping the fun alive after her passing."

"Fun. Yeah." I still had brambles in my jeans. "What did Daniel say about that vial?"

She made a face. "It's got my magic on it, but Daniel says the vial is circumstantial evidence." She waved her hand like it was nonsense. "It's possible I left my magical signature doing the usual bookkeeping. He thinks that, and maybe pushing the police to compare my potion to the one used on Maria, might give me a good shot of getting off."

"When's your court date?"

"They're figuring all that out. Wouldn't be here

though. Daniel says all the criminal stuff for the supernaturals gets funneled to a single court in New Orleans, so there's a backlog. Might be next year before they bring me up on charges."

"Good," I said. "Plenty of time for us to figure out who really did it."

She turned to me, brows raised as she finally retrieved the bottle she was looking for. "You... I think Vinnie can handle that, don't you?"

"I think he wants Pinfish off his tail, pun intended," I said, following her out to the bar and sidling up next to her.

"You're really serious about this, aren't you?" she asked. "Did you ever work the bar when you were younger?" She paused. "No, of course not. You were only eighteen."

"I'm a quick study." After all, I learned clients' content management systems every day. How difficult could tending bar be?

Chapter Ten

"Go get that."

"No, not that."

"Why did you get three? I asked for one."

It turned out, tending bar with Aimee was a lot harder than anticipated. For one, I hadn't a clue where anything was located or what we had on hand. For another, I couldn't make any Witchwhackers or any other liquor-based drinks because I didn't want to end up at another crime scene by using Big Jo's wand. And finally, my *small* attempts to make the process more efficient (such as grabbing two beers from the back when someone ordered one, so I'd be ready for the next customer) were met with derision.

"Just go clean up," Aimee snapped, finally. "And get out of my way before I hex you."

It was hard not to remind Aimee that, until we sorted through Big Jo's estate, this place was mine to oversee. But I was sure if I did, she'd walk out the door, and I'd have a bar full of thirsty supernaturals and no way to serve them.

With a grimace, I grabbed a rag and bucket and headed out into the bustling bar. This sort of work could've been done by a wand—or a Cove kid... except Big Jo hadn't wanted them working past sundown. That, and there was usually a second, more talented witch to help manage the chaos. Since I wasn't that, I picked up beer bottles, wiped down empty tables, and, where needed, delivered the errant hot dog or burger to a table before zipping on.

It felt very different from the night of my grandmother's memorial. For one thing, I wasn't being recognized left and right. And for another, there were definitely more *types* of supernaturals than I was used to here. Besides the few witches, there were werewolves and a few vampires, (no mermaids, I noted with a grimace), but also elves with pointed ears and long, slick hair who looked like they'd walked off a catwalk in Sweden. Fairies the size of my palm flittered about, leaving dust in their wake. In the corner, what I could only assume was a centaur was drinking a beer with another ogre who could've been Kit's uncle for all I knew.

"How long has it been like this?" I asked Aimee, as I dropped off another set of glasses to be washed.

"Like what?" she asked, still a little annoyance still in her voice.

"All these different kinds of creatures," I said. "I thought we were a witch bar."

"You can thank your friend Cal for that," she said, sliding over a freshly grilled hamburger. "Take this to Stuart."

"He's not my friend—" I began, but she hustled away to serve a pair of elves a Witchwhacker. I held the burger, glaring at her, before turning on my heel to find the ferry owner.

He wasn't too far, sitting on the edge of the bar and looking like he wanted to keep his distance from everyone.

When I approached, his eyes lit up. "Well, look at you, wearing a Cove shirt and making an honest living," he said, taking the burger from me. "Big Jo would be proud."

"I'm not so sure about that," I said with a shake of my head as I leaned on the table. "How was your day? Mine's been absolute garbage."

"Sit down, kiddo," Stuart said, offering me the seat across from him.

"Boss might get mad if I take a break," I said,

nodding to Aimee, who seemed in her element as she bounced from person to person. "Wouldn't know she was arrested earlier today for murder."

"Ridiculous," he said. "I'm sure they'll clear her name in no time."

"You're in and out of the water all the time," I said. "Any idea who might've had it in for Maria?"

He shook his head. "The mermaids leave me alone, by and large. I got a few charms on the boat to catch any trash before it goes into the water. Engines are powered by magic, so that makes the merfolk happy."

At least someone was.

"Busy night," I said, nodding to the crowd behind us. "I don't recognize a single person except you."

"Yeah, been trending that way the last few years," he said, and didn't sound too upset about it.

"I mean, I knew that Eldred's Beach has been drawing in the supernaturals, but I thought they stayed on their side of things. Especially considering the time it takes to get here."

"Who'd pass up an opportunity to visit the Eldred's Hollow institution?" Stuart said with a chuckle. "I think a lot of them are curious about the place. The witches who work across the sound talk a lot about it. Builds up in their minds. Then they come to find it's a simple dive bar, but when they try the drinks, they're sold. The Witchwhacker is world-renowned, you know."

I seriously doubted that, but it was the kind of hyperbole folks in Eldred's Hollow liked to spew. Still, I chanced another look around, not liking how unfamiliar everyone was. When I was a kid, I could name every person who walked under the awning. Aimee didn't seem to mind. Perhaps she'd gotten used to it.

Or, I thought with a nasty grimace, *maybe she realizes that money is money, and we need as much as we can get.*

"Gotta get back to it," I told Stuart.

"You should come on the ferry one of these days," he said. "Check out what's going on across the sound."

"Why would I do that when I have paradise right here?" I said, picking up the bucket and heading toward a table that had gotten up to leave. After clearing that, I ping-ponged between tables, even chancing getting a replacement beer for the centaur when he asked for one. Aimee's gaze was on me as I retrieved a *single* beer (which I made sure to show her) and dropped it off.

"Jo?"

Karen was clearly having a girls' night with a couple of witches I thought I recognized. She looked less like a mom tonight and more like a twenty-something, with a tight black top and dark jeans.

"Hey," I said, walking up to her. "You look

nice."

"Thanks. My mom has the kids." She let out a sigh that told me she *lived* for these nights.

"What are you drinking?" I asked.

"Give me a Witchwhacker."

I turned to make the drink, but Aimee was already bringing one to her. "Evening, Karen."

"Aimee. Glad to see you're back." She took a long swig of the drink and let out another contented sigh. "That hits the spot."

"Thanks," I said to Aimee's retreating back, but I couldn't be sure she'd heard me.

"So, are you working here now?" Karen asked.

"Trying to help Aimee out," I said. "Doesn't feel like I'm doing much in that department."

"Aimee's got this place down to a science. Even Big Jo had to stay out of her way sometimes." She took another sip. "Though I'm surprised to see her here. You know, after she was arrested. Do you know the details?"

"They found some circumstantial evidence," I said. "Daniel doesn't think it'll stand up in court. Whenever that is."

"Daniel. What a change in him, eh?" She chuckled. "Man goes to law school and comes out all confident and... well, not blond."

"I don't mind blond," I said, almost a little absentmindedly, earning a curious look from Karen. "But he's been invaluable. Helping with Big Jo's estate and all that. And now with Aimee, I—"

My attention diverted as Carver Briggs swaggered through the door, wearing a popped-collar shirtand linen shorts. To my surprise, he was with the same attractive woman he'd been with the night before. She batted her long eyelashes at him as he loudly chatted with his fellow werewolves, and he very possessively draped his arm around her. Nobody in the group looked even remotely emotional about Maria's death.

"Huh."

"What?" Karen asked.

"Who's that girl Carver's with?" I asked.

"Oh, that's Natasha Lunaris." She took a sip of her beer. "Why? You interested?"

"Interested in why they're looking like it's just another Friday night when his ex-girlfriend was found murdered on my beach yesterday," I said. "How long have they been together?"

"Couple weeks, I guess. After Maria got promoted," Karen said, "she dumped him."

"So I hear. And I also heard he was torn up about it," I said. "Doesn't seem that way now."

"No, it doesn't." Karen had to shake her head as the two wolves shared an intimate kiss. "But you know Carver. He's a player."

"Supposedly, he's got an alibi," I replied. "So Vinnie says."

"Are you taking up the investigation?" Karen

asked with a grin.

"Just curious." I leaned in. "So what's her deal? His girlfriend? I don't remember her hanging around here."

"Nah, she's a second cousin or grandniece or something like that to Big Dog," she said.

I made a face. "Wouldn't that make her related to Carver?"

"You know those wolves. They're big on incest, so I hear." She chuckled. "Natasha somehow got out of working at the grocery, too. She's helping Tom at the co-op."

"Wonder how she managed that?" Big Dog liked to keep his pack close.

"Guess he likes her," she said. "Not sure what brought her here, but she's clearly happy with her choices. Can't imagine Big Dog's too mad with that pairing, either. Probably terrified Carver was going to end up with a witch or a mermaid."

"Do you think it's that serious?" I asked.

"I mean, it's Carver," Karen said with a small laugh. "He goes through women like tissue paper. We all thought it was a big deal when he and Maria were an item, because they were together for at least eight months."

"And now he's with Natasha."

"To be honest, there was a *bit* of talk about how fast they hooked up after he and Maria called it quits. Some said he was already seeing Natasha on the side before Maria dumped him. I mean, the woman lived in the sea. Not as if she could keep an eye on her man every second from there."

"Suppose not." I, personally, didn't want to date anyone I couldn't trust to keep his wand in his pants. "Hey, listen, you said you got into potion-making, right?"

She nodded. "Mostly cleaning. Why?"

"Do people around here tend to make their own or buy it?" I asked.

"Depends on what it is." She sat back. "Why?"

I debated revealing all my cards. But I didn't know a way to ask the question without it. "What about that mermaid-stunning potion?"

She licked her lips. "Well, that is...kind of a complex one. And also, your grandmother forbade anyone who comes to her shores from using it. So that tends to make it a little harder to find in Eldred's Hollow."

"What about on the beach?" I asked.

"It's supposedly the same over there, too," Karen said. "But maybe I could ask around. Though I'm sure if someone had a vial, they aren't advertising it." She leaned in. "Does that mean I can be part of your investigation?"

"It's not an investigation," I said with a sigh. "I'm trying to help clear Aimee's name."

"Maybe you should ask her where she got hers, hm? After all, if she's got nothing to hide, she shouldn't have a problem telling you."

I turned to watch the bar. "Good idea."

Fridays went late, and I was dead on my feet before last call. But I dutifully hung around until every last supernatural was out the door. Aimee tapped her wand against the outside pole, and the garage door-like windows shuttered closed and locked with a click.

"That's how you lock up, by the way," she said, pointedly.

"You know I can't do that," I said.

"Then why are you here?"

She marched back to the bar to continue tidying up, which for her, meant tapping the bar with her wand. One rag wiped up all the condensation rings, while a spray bottle floated behind that, spritzing the bar with cleaning solution, and another rag zipped after, wiping up the spritz. Once that passed, the stool beneath the bar flipped upside-down on top of the bar, and a broom swept by with a dustpan.

"I'm here because this is my grandmother's place," I said, after a long pause.

Aimee let out a snort, and my anger boiled over.

"What's your problem?" I snapped.

"My problem is you left this place unattended. The office door unlocked. The wrong person showed up, and we could've been robbed. You know we need every penny we make. How could you be so careless?"

My face burned. "I wasn't trying to be careless. I couldn't lock up, and I just ran home for a few minutes. The Shack had other plans." I cleared my throat. "I left Jimbo in charge."

As if on cue, the seagull familiar swooped in and landed on the Witchwhacker machine, demanding food. When neither of us obliged, he took flight to his nest at the top of the rafters then settled in and fell asleep.

Aimee quirked a brow at me.

"Okay, so it wasn't my brightest idea, but I really thought I'd be back quickly," I said.

She let out a sigh as she opened the cash register and said nothing.

"I'm sorry, okay?"

"I was arrested today, Jo," she said quietly, counting the cash without looking at me. "But you know the one thing I kept thinking about? What was gonna happen to this place. I loved your grandmother like a sister."

I nodded. "I know."

"If I'm not here to keep it running, I'd hoped, at least, you'd have the…" She sighed, closing the register and putting the cash in an envelope. "Never mind."

"If it were up to me, you'd have this place," I said. "But you know it's more complicated than that." I nodded to the envelope she was tucking under her arm. "Good night?"

"Awful," she said. "The lack of mermaid business is going to kill us if it keeps up. Good thing nobody robbed us while the front door was unlocked."

"You're seriously not going to let that go?" I snapped as she walked by me, broomstick in hand. "I. Can't. Do. Magic. Ergo, I can't lock the doors."

"Then maybe you should practice more."

"And I'll end up turning my hair purple or electrocuting myself or setting a bush on fire. Ask me how I know." All things I vividly remembered doing as a child.

"I'm going home. It's been a long day," she said, walking toward the door.

She was halfway there before I asked her the question I'd been hoping to ask all night. "Where do you get your mermaid-stunning potion?"

She stopped, mid-step. "What?"

"Where do you get the potion from?" I asked, turning to her. "The one everyone says you carry around all the time."

"You mean this?" She reached into her pocket and pulled out her mermaid-stunning potion.

"Yeah, that. The one that implicated you in the crime." I couldn't believe she still had it on her. "Why do you still have it? Didn't the police take it from you?"

"No." She chuckled and put it away. "It's not technically illegal. Big Jo didn't have that kind of power."

"Maybe you should think about leaving it at home," I said.

"Are you kidding? I'm currently enemy number one with the mermaids," she said, glaring at me. "It's best to be prepared."

Okay, I could give her that. "Where do you get it?"

"I made it myself," she said, looking at the vial. "Not that the police believed me, but this is all I have. One vial. After Gracie's father died, I researched how to make it, sourced the ingredients, and fashioned it myself." She pocketed it again. "I've never used it, though. Obviously."

"So you have no idea where someone would've gotten the stuff that killed Maria?" I asked.

"I mean, I do have an idea." She pointed toward the shore, or, more specifically, the twinkling lights in the distance. "Wouldn't put it past the folks on the other side of the sound to have it on hand and lie about it. They tend to talk out of both sides of their fangs, you know."

"I suppose you told Vinnie that," I said softly.

"I did. Clearly, he didn't believe me." She shook her head. "Daniel believes I've got a good case. Says he can refer me to some of his friends who do this sort of thing on the regular, but he'll advise me until

I can nail one down. But they're gonna cost an arm and a leg, and I don't have that kind of money." She paused and eyed me as I opened my mouth. "And don't say you'll pay for it, because the Cove can't afford to hire me one either."

"I don't know how, but I'm gonna fix all this," I said. "Get your name cleared. Get the mermaids back. Find the missing money. I promise you, I'm not going to leave you in the lurch."

"I wish I could believe you," she said. "Actions speak louder than words, though. Big Jo never would've left this place unattended. And if you cared, you wouldn't have either."

And with that, she walked out the door, hopped on her broom, and flew off into the night.

I stood in the bar, the whirring of the Witchwhacker machine the only sound as my promise to Aimee echoed in my ears.

Chapter Eleven

The next morning, The Shack decided to rouse me with a wonderful game where it lifted and lowered the floorboards under the couch until I sat up.

"I'm awake, you infernal house," I barked. It was only nine, and my too-late evening last night had ended a mere five hours ago.

The cabinets shook, and the carafe rattled. The Shack wanted me to know it had made coffee.

"Do you want a medal?" I said, crabby from lack of sleep.

The floorboards beneath the couch raised, and

the entire thing tipped forward, sending me sprawling onto the floor.

"Very funny."

I did, in fact, thank The Shack for brewing coffee, as well as for the assortment of fruit I ate for breakfast. I didn't feel like showing my face at the Enchanted Cat again, especially when it would probably be much busier than usual. Saturday mornings usually were.

Instead, I found one of Big Jo's telephone bills so I could inquire about DSL with the service provider. An hour on hold later, I reached a lovely representative who informed me that everything was all set up for internet, I just needed to buy the equipment. The price direct was outrageous, so I declined and told her I'd pick one up elsewhere. The closest big box store was over an hour away, close to Mobile, but I had a hunch I might be able to find one closer.

I found the text that had alerted me to my grandmother's death and called the number. I wanted to ask Daniel some other questions, too—about Aimee, and what I should do next—but I was also pretty sure he'd know where I could score a modem that wouldn't send me all the way to Mobile.

The answer was groggy. "Mm'lo."

"D-Daniel?" I was taken aback. It was nearly eleven. "Sorry, did I wake you?"

"Yes." The bed shifted under him through the line. "What's up?"

"I...uh..." I doubted he wanted to discuss Aimee's case so early in his day, so I opted for the mundane question. "Do you know where I can get a DSL modem in town?"

There was a long pause. "I'm sorry?"

I winced, hating that I'd woken him up for something so simple. "I'm sorry I woke you. Just wondering if you know where—"

"Co-op."

"Right." Should've thought of that. "Sorry about—" I cleared my throat. "Thanks. Go back to sleep."

He grunted, and the line went dead.

I stared at the phone, hoping his gruffness was because I'd woken him and not because he was angry with me.

Not that it mattered, of course. He could not like me and still offer legal advice.

"Anyway." I announced to no one, shaking myself, "to the co-op."

Since most witches didn't like to mingle with the non-magical folks if they could help it, a co-op had sprung up in the center of town that could provide anything and everything a person needed from the outside world that they couldn't conjure by magic. It also sold magical feed for the specialized livestock in town, gas for regular cars, and all manner of kitsch to fill a home with unique trinkets. One could find a little bit of everything there, from plugs and light switches to fenders, wagon wheels, and fence posts. I wasn't sure how Tom Canard, the owner of the co-op, sourced his products, but I had a hunch he spent a lot of time at the antique shops that dotted Highway 98.

The store was in the same cluster of buildings as everything else in town, a little north of the main intersection where the cafe, wand shop, bank, and apothecary sat. I pulled into one of the two parking spots. To my left, the gas pump showed a price nearly a dollar cheaper than anywhere else in the country. On the front porch, under the awning, several white rocking chairs moved in the light breeze underneath dancing wind chimes. A plastic pink flamingo sat by the front steps, next to a large stone turtle wearing a saddle and small white cowboy hat.

I jumped as it moved its head to look at me before extending its neck to chomp off a piece of grass.

Not stone, then.

I walked by it, keeping my distance as it watched me with beady eyes, not slowing until I was safely inside the co-op.

The place seemed even bigger than I remembered. A maze of shelves welcomed me, some holding large plastic bins with smaller items inside. Organization wasn't the co-op's strong suit, as there was a collection of light switches next to a blue magical flame that could be purchased to heat a cauldron. On the shelf above, another plastic bin with door hinges sat next to a large glass jar containing unicorn hair. The corner display showed a stack of *Farmer's Almanac* books for this year, and next to that was a fish tank filled with large black spiders climbing over each other.

After wandering a bit, I finally reached the back counter where I'd find someone to help me. No one was there, but there was a sign that said, *"Speak what you need."*

"Uh...modem?" I called to the space.

"Who are you talking to?"

I spun around, finding myself face-to-face with Natasha, who was wearing a name tag on her t-shirt and a pair of jeans that accentuated everything. She held a box of screwdrivers, each with a little tag on them. I cleared my throat and tried to brush off my embarrassment.

"Just looking for a modem," I said, gesturing to the sign. "Thought the sign was—"

"It's tongue-in-cheek," she said. "There's not a charm or anything on the place. It means I'm here to get it for you if you don't have a wand." She put her hand on her hip and gave me a once-over. "But aren't you a witch?"

Should I have been grateful she hadn't recognized me? "Yes and no—"

"Oh, right. I remember you." Drat. "You're the magicless witch. Big Jo's granddaughter. Carver told me *all* about you."

I wasn't sure I wanted to know what kind of stories he was telling. "That's me."

"Surprised you're sticking around. What with the trouble at the Cove." She smirked, brushing past me. "Heard your bartender was arrested."

She dumped the screwdrivers in a bin clearly marked *nails*. I opened my mouth to ask if she knew the difference, but based on her bored expression, I doubted she'd care even if she did.

"T-that's right," I said. "But they've got the wrong person."

"I'm sure you do." She picked up a spider that had crawled out and tossed it in with the unicorn hair. I was beginning to see why she hadn't been offered a job with the rest of the werewolves. "You guys were there that night. Did you see anything?"

She lifted a perfectly plucked eyebrow at me. "Did we see anything?"

"I mean, Carver *left* with—"

"And Carver's been cleared by the police." She turned to me, hands on her hips. "Why are you asking?"

"Just making conversation," I said, hoping she'd buy it.

Based on her scowl, she didn't. "Did you need something?"

"Yes, a modem, if you have one. For a DSL connection," I said.

"I'll see what we have."

She disappeared, and I doubted she was going to look for what I'd asked for. I stood at the help counter for a few minutes before turning to go find her. Instead, I ran into the owner, Tom, a short, black man wearing a well-loved, stained apron. He let out a cry of happiness when he saw me and swept me into a bear hug that left me breathless.

"Meant to give you that the other night," he said, releasing me. "You looked like a deer in headlights."

"Felt like it," I said. "Good to see you, Tom. How's business?"

"Busier than ever," he said, picking up a small branch that held a hanging bat and putting it on top of a shelf. "Especially with all the folks passing through on their way to Eldred's Beach."

"They do that?" I asked.

"Well, they're taking the ferry," he said. "Need to gas up their car. Stop in here to see what I've got."

I craned my neck, spotting a collection of shiny dragon scales sitting next to three cans of motor oil. "You've certainly expanded the place."

"Everything in here is something someone's

come in asking for," he said. "We keep adding."

"Do you have a DSL modem?" I asked.

"Of course we do." He pulled his wand and waved it in the air. Moments later, a small black box appeared with an electrical cord attached to it. "On the house."

"Oh, I insist on paying for it," I said.

"You're family, Little Jo. Besides that, I hear you've got enough to be getting on with at the Cove, what with Maria's death and Aimee and all the madness there."

"News travels fast." I tucked the box under my arm as Natasha whirled around the corner.

She took one look at me and her boss and turned and ran in the other direction.

"That girl," Tom muttered. "Doing Big Dog a favor, hiring her on. I told him I didn't have much use for a magicless helper here, and the Fates know she doesn't give a cat's hair about keeping this place in order."

That Tom considered it "in order" was surprising. "She seems...nice."

"Pain in the rear is what she is. I think her eyes are going to get stuck if she rolls them at me one more time."

"How long has she worked here?"

He blew air between his lips. "A month. Seems like longer, though. She lasted two weeks at the grocery."

"She's seeing Carver Briggs, right?" I said with a smile. "Maybe you'll get lucky, and he'll marry her and take her off your hands." She seemed like the kind who wanted to be kept by a rich spouse.

He chuckled. "Maybe. But even Carver's got to get tired of her bad attitude. She's from New Orleans. Thinks she's too big for this town, and perhaps she is. Definitely didn't waste any time snapping up the richest guy in town, and if you ask me, she's getting impatient that he hasn't proposed."

"I thought he was dating Maria up until recently?" I asked.

"Oh yeah," he said. "But you know how some people are. Natasha's got her eyes on the prize." His face softened. "Such a shame what happened to Maria. Never really talked to her much myself, but I always heard nice things about her."

"Carver didn't seem too upset about it," I said, glancing around to make sure Natasha wasn't nearby. I didn't know how well werewolves could hear, but I hoped Tom would give me some of that good Eldred's Hollow gossip. "Saw him last night at the Cove, and he seemed practically giddy."

"You don't think he...?"

"I don't know. But I know Aimee didn't do it, and I seem to be the only one in town who thinks so," I said.

"Carver's a snooty fellow, but a murderer?" He

shook his head. "Not when he was moping around after Maria when she dumped him. It was easy for Natasha to snap him up."

Was it jealousy?

Perhaps it wasn't Carver who'd killed her, but Natasha. I could see a situation where Maria and Carver were thinking of getting back together, and Natasha saw her way out of town being taken away.

A loud crash echoed from the back room, and Tom sighed. "Guess I'd better go see what she's broken this time."

"Good luck," I said. "And thanks for the modem."

~

Sweet, glorious internet.

Within half an hour of returning to The Shack, I was sitting on the back porch with a glass of sweet tea, working through my emails. They were all so mundane compared to the chaos of Eldred's Hollow. An email from a client who wanted to redo all the metadata tags I'd painstakingly developed with them. Another client who didn't understand the difference between a filtered view of their data and a folder. A reminder email to submit my hours for the week.

I whittled the five hundred emails down to the fifty that I needed to take action on, firing off messages to clients to let them know that I was still out of pocket and dealing with my grandmother's affairs. And while I could've tackled the outstanding tasks, instead, I put my laptop down and took in the view for a moment.

"You look awfully at home."

Kit stood at the bottom of the stairs, wearing her Enchanted Cat Cafe shirt and a pair of jeans, and smiling up at me.

"Nice and quiet out here," I said, nodding to the empty rocking chair. "Have a seat. You're probably tired."

"You said it." She climbed the stairs and sat next to me, stretching out in the afternoon sun and smiling. "Oh, this is lovely." She pointed her wand at my tea, refilling it and creating one of her own. "Lovely, lovely."

"What brings you out this way?" I asked.

"Tom said you'd popped in," she said. "Asking about Natasha."

"Why were you talking with Tom?"

"Oh, you know the Eldred's Hollow scuttlebutt," she said. "He came in for lunch. Knew we were friends. Wanted to make sure I knew you were in town. Told him we'd chatted. He wanted me to check on you. So," she gestured to herself, "here I am."

"I forgot how quickly news moves in this town," I said.

"So why were you asking about Natasha?" She wagged her brow. "Jealous of Carver's new girl?"

"Wondering if they had anything to do with Maria's death," I said, rocking slowly in the chair as I surveyed the grassy field beyond.

Kit stopped rocking. "Wait, really? Vinnie's got a handle on that, you know."

"Vinnie thinks it's Aimee. And I have a feeling he's getting pressure to focus on her and nothing else." I kept my gaze on the field. "Whether from Big Dog or the mermaids, something isn't adding up. Danny said—"

"Oh, *Danny*," she said with a coo.

"What about him?" I finally turned to look at her.

She screwed up her face and lowered her voice. "*Let's go.*"

"What's that supposed to mean?" I asked, my cheeks heating.

"Just that I thought it was cute that he sprang into action for you," she said, adjusting herself in the rocking chair. "He's kind of like that, you know. Likes to help out where he can. But I think he's taken a *special* interest in you."

"I doubt that." Especially after the gruff way he answered the phone.

"Jo, he had the *biggest* crush on you growing up."

I blanched. "Did he really?"

"Big one. He'd never admit to it, but he'd get so tongue-tied when you were around." She chuckled.

"Such a sweet boy he was."

"I'm pretty sure that ship has sailed," I said. "I called him this morning, and you would've thought I'd offended him on a spiritual level."

"Oh, yeah? Hard to do that. He's pretty even-keeled."

"You didn't hear him when I called."

"What time did you call?"

I shrugged. "Eleven, maybe?"

"Yeah, that'll do it." She snickered. "He's not what you call a morning person. He's barely human before one on the weekends."

"Isn't he a…lawyer?" I asked with a laugh.

"Yeah, but he works for himself, so he keeps different hours," she said. "I'm sure if you called him now, he'd be all smiles for you."

I didn't like the direction of this conversation, so I wanted to change it. "I do appreciate him helping Aimee out, though. At least he was able to get her out the same night. He seems confident she's got a good case. But I can't really trust Vinnie. I get the feeling he's just trying to bury this as quickly as possible."

"It's a bit…strange he's zeroed in on Aimee," Kit said. "Especially as there were tons of folks at the Cove that night."

I nodded. "Carver, Natasha. Some random tourists I've never seen before. Aimee, you, me. The regulars."

"Any one of them could have a motive," Kit said, before tutting. "Listen to us. Talking like a couple of biddies on *Murder, She Wrote*."

"Classic show," I said, giving her a look. "Anyway. Carver and Maria were arguing the night of Big Jo's funeral, *and* she was the last person I saw him with. So how in the world could he have an alibi that's believable?"

"You told Vinnie all this, didn't you?" Kit asked.

I nodded. "The night of the murder, he seemed receptive. The next day? Not so much. That's why I think someone or something is pressuring him to find a scapegoat." My phone buzzed with a reminder that I needed to get ready to go soon.

"Got a hot date?" Kit asked.

"Helping Aimee out at the Cove," I said. "Not that I was much help last night."

"Look at you, running over to tend bar," she said. "Don't tell me you're moving back."

I glanced at my closed laptop beside me. There could be a world where I worked from here, managed the bar, and lived a simpler life. But that world required me to be something I wasn't.

"The Shack wouldn't let me stay," I said. "It's a miracle it hasn't eaten the internet connection yet."

The sentient house groaned behind me, as if warning that I shouldn't trust it.

"Well, in any case, I'm happy to see you back. We'll be at the diner bright and early on Monday if you want to stop in for breakfast." She grinned. "Can't promise Daniel will be there, but—"

"Thanks." I rolled my eyes. "I'll see if The Shack wants to wake me up with buttered toast to the face again."

At her perplexed look, I shook my head.

"Never mind."

Chapter Twelve

By the time I pulled into the parking lot, it was already almost full, and the dull roar of a band was echoing across the open air. The beach was littered with boats of all sizes—some empty, some with people sitting on them and rocking out with plastic cups in their hand. But I couldn't help but notice the lack of mermaids in the water joining them.

I made my way across the deck and into the bar itself, finding it packed to the gills. Every kind of supernatural creature was there, from the usual witches and werewolves to demons, centaurs, elves, satyrs, and more than a few vamps who could be identified by their distinct lack of drink.

Aimee was in her element, whipping up drinks and grinning as she'd been the night before. Grace was helping her, and together, the two of them were a vision. I tried to ignore the way it hurt to see them use their wands with ease—one of them conjuring up a drink, another tapping it to add the signature Witchwhacker color. They were of one mind, and more importantly, one magic.

"Nice of you to show up," Aimee said, giving me a look. "We open at ten on Saturdays, in case you forgot."

I winced. I had forgotten. "You should have called."

"Clearly we have it covered." She glared at me as she continued past me. "Go home."

Even Grace was glaring at me as if I'd committed the ultimate sin. Then again, I'm sure she'd been roped in to help her mother at the last minute.

"I'm sorry." I picked up the empty dish bucket. "I'll get to cleaning up."

Aimee's gaze was on me as I canvassed the room, but now wasn't the time to get into an in-depth conversation about her feelings.

"Trouble at Witch's Cove?"

I spun around, narrowing my gaze and already reflexively reaching for the wand I probably shouldn't use. Lewis was standing at the table to my right, a drink in hand, and no camera or pen in sight. I relaxed, only a little, as it did look like he was having a drink after work and not looking for the next scoop.

"Nothing you need to write about." I glared at him as I snatched the empty beer bottle from the table and added it to the rest of them.

"Peace, Jo." He held up his hands. "I'm here enjoying the band. No stories happening tonight."

"Unless you sniff one out."

"Oh, why so sullen?" He smiled, but it did nothing to endear him to me. "Bad day? Heard you were asking around about Natasha and Carver."

"I thought you weren't writing any stories tonight?" I asked. "And how does *everyone* know my business?"

"It's Eldred's Hollow," he said with a chuckle. "Everybody knows everything about everybody. That's the beauty and burden of living in a small town."

He could say that twice.

"I was at the co-op getting a modem so I can do my job from The Shack, considering it looks like I won't be going anywhere anytime soon."

"That's good to hear."

Daniel appeared from the crowd carrying two bottles of beer. He handed one to Lewis and sidled up to the table beside him, smiling at me. For a moment, I remembered what Kit had said about him having a crush on me then I realized who he was having a drink with.

"You two are friends?"

"You say that like it's a bad thing," Lewis said. "Not *everyone* in town thinks I'm the scum of the earth, you know."

I pursed my lips, glaring at him. I'd have to be much more careful about what I told Daniel in the future if he was friendly with Lewis.

"Is there something wrong, Jo?" Daniel asked.

"Nothing." I adjusted the bucket of dirty dishes against my hip. "Thanks for the info this morning."

Daniel stared at me as if I had two heads. "What info?"

"I called you…" I said slowly.

"You did?" He blinked, his eyes wide and a little blush appearing on his cheeks beneath his beard. "When?"

Lewis laughed as Daniel pulled out his phone and presumably looked for the recent calls.

"Was it before one?" Lewis asked.

I nodded.

"Well, that's your problem. Daniel doesn't exist before one for anyone."

"Shoot. Sorry Jo." He put his phone away and shook his head. "I honestly don't remember any of that."

"I mean, it's fine. I was calling about…" Well, I was calling about a lot of things. But none of them I wanted to discuss in front of Lewis, who'd put it on the front page of the paper at the first chance he could get. "Where I could get a modem. Anyway." I adjusted the bucket again. "Back to work."

I kept my distance from the two of them, though Daniel watched me as I dashed around. I didn't know what to make of their friendship and was more than a little annoyed Kit had put the idea that he'd had a crush in my mind.

The night wore on, and the band kept playing, the sound echoing over the water. Boats came and went, and I took over collecting their rental payments, where needed. I ferried beer and Witchwhackers and other drinks when Aimee was too busy to, and carried the remnants back. I washed dishes by hand and restocked. All the while, I didn't dare speak with Aimee unless I was asking how to do something.

Around eleven, the band stopped playing, replaced by the dull roar of the speakers and conversation. Sometime during the evening, Daniel and Lewis left. I'd have to get the story of their friendship from Kit tomorrow.

"Waitress—"

I spun around, coming face to face with Natasha and Carver, who'd taken over the table Lewis and Daniel had vacated. She recognized me, her eyes growing wide then narrowing.

"Oh, it's you again," she said, disdain dripping

from her upturned lip.

"Well, it is my bar," I replied with a smile I didn't feel. But they were customers, and maybe if I was nice, they might let something slip.

"*Your* bar?" Carver gave me a once-over. "Really?

"Big Jo left it to me," I said, though that wasn't *technically* true yet. "Why is that surprising?"

"Because you're a witch without magic," he said. "What are you going to do with a bar that runs on it?"

"Hire people with magic, obviously," I said, my smile hard to keep now. "You haven't changed one bit, Carver. Still trying to fill a pair of britches that are hopelessly too big for you."

"And you're better off playing like you're a regular human," he replied. "Because that's all you're gonna be. This bar is going under and—"

"Where did you and Maria go the night of her murder?" I asked, hoping to catch him off guard.

"Why do you want to know?" Natasha asked when Carver didn't answer quickly enough. "Are you some kind of investigator now?"

"The murder happened at my bar," I said.

"I already cleared it with Vinnie," he said, rubbing his nose. "Got an alibi."

"Oh yeah?" I put one hand on my hip. "You left with her the night she died."

"Yeah? They had a quick chat. Then Tasha and I left and went to Grouper. It's a very *posh* restaurant at the top of the Grand Oceanview Resort," Natasha said, pulling out her phone. "Since you're so *nosy*, here's the damn proof."

She shoved her phone in my face, revealing a slew of Instagram posts dated from two nights ago. They were tagged at a restaurant over in Eldred's Beach, about an hour after I'd last seen them.

"What does this prove? You could've killed her before you headed over there?"

"Not that it's *any* of your business, but the cops pinned her death at ten," Natasha said, pointing to the last photo. "We were eating dessert then. Obviously, they checked our alibis. I know this is a backwater, podunk town, but the police would think twice about casting suspicion on the local werewolf alpha's *favorite* son."

"I'd think they'd cast suspicion on anyone who might be responsible," I shot back, glaring at them.

She yanked her phone back. "Honestly, Carver, why do we come to this dump, anyway? We should be at the beach where a higher caliber of people hang out."

Carver didn't look like he wholeheartedly agreed, but he grabbed his keys off the counter. "Let's go."

~

Carver took his contingent of werewolves with him, and considering the dire straits the bar was in, it probably hadn't been the wisest idea to run him off. I'd wanted so badly for Carver or Natasha to be the culprits, if only so I could tell Aimee the good news. But neither one of them could magic themselves back from Eldred's Beach so fast—even if they'd wanted to. And I was sure Vinnie had checked their alibis with the folks at the hotel.

Which meant we were back to square one.

The crowd finally dwindled to a few very drunk stragglers, which Aimee shooed onto a couple of waiting broomsticks outside. I was surprised to see the sober witches at the ready, but it was, perhaps, a smart way to earn some easy cash on a Saturday night.

"What a night," I said, returning to the empty bar. "How'd we do?"

"Do you care?"

I threw my hands in the air. "I think you know the answer to that question, Aimee. For goodness sake. I've been here—"

"Since four. The bar opened—"

"I got it," I snapped. "I'll do better tomorrow. Be here bright and early at ten."

"You'll be the only one here. We don't open until noon on Sundays. Blue laws." The chairs hopped onto the bar as they had the night before.

I watched them, unwilling to rehash the same apologies I'd already given her.

"It's a lot by myself," Aimee said, after all the stools were up on the counter. "Big Jo and I used to... Well, we'd divide and conquer. She'd manage the marina, I'd tend bar. But without her..."

I watched her, sensing that she hadn't even had a chance to grieve yet.

"I'm not Big Jo," I said quietly. "I don't have her talent or her tenacity or her way with people."

"I know you aren't. But...." She nodded toward me, and I assumed it was the wand still stuck in my bra strap. "I didn't see you pull that thing out once."

"I don't know how else to say I can't do magic, Aimee," I said, almost a little helplessly.

"You won't try."

"I did try. Ended up staring at a dead mermaid."

She snorted. "You tried to do something big. Opening and closing the bar isn't big. It's easy. Simple. Tap tap of the wand." As if proving a point, she tapped the nearest pole, and all the doors rolled down. "I know you don't think you can do it, but if you don't even attempt it, you never will."

"That's what Big Jo used to say to me," I said.

"And she was right." She put a hand on her hip as she watched me. "What in the world were you doing today, anyway? Heard several people say—"

"That I was asking about Natasha and Carver?" I shook my head as I stared at the ceiling. "Word gets around."

"Well?"

"I'm trying to figure out if they had anything to

do with Maria's death," I said.

"Vinnie said—"

"Vinnie can't be trusted," I snapped. "At least, I don't think he can. It seemed too... I don't know. Carver always had a short fuse. Natasha seems like she's willing to do whatever it takes to get what she wants." I paused, staring at the weathered wooden floor. "Maybe she was jealous and decided to make sure Maria couldn't ever steal her man."

Aimee chuckled humorlessly. "I suppose that's possible."

"Natasha said the police determined the time of death to be around ten. But I can't shake the idea that maybe someone's hiding something. What if the time of death was much earlier, but they said it was ten to give the werewolf an alibi?"

"You're sounding a bit paranoid," Aimee said. "And I'm the one who's being charged with murder." She seemed to lose some of her anger as she finished counting the cash and put it into the envelope, tucking it under her arm. "I appreciate you looking into this, but...Daniel says we're good. You don't need to worry about me."

"Yeah, can we trust Daniel?" I asked.

Aimee laughed. "What's that supposed to mean?"

"He's friends with Lewis." I made a face. "I thought he was on our side."

"Friends is a stretch," Aimee said. "Drinking

buddies is more like it. I wouldn't look too much into it. Especially after all the help he's given me—and you." She conjured her broom. "Well, I'm headed out for the evening. Do you want to finish up in here?"

The answer should've been no. All the trash bags still needed to be emptied, and I was bone tired. I pulled out Big Jo's wand and sighed. "Sure would be nice if this thing worked, you know?"

"Taking the trash out is simple enough," she said, walking to the door. "Big Jo did it thousands of times. Bet her wand barely needs a suggestion to do it."

With that, she hopped on her broom and left.

I held the wand and let her words roll around in my mind. For most witches, magic was like breathing. A wand was used to concentrate the power and give it direction, but even the tiniest witches could cast and summon without needing a complex set of incantations.

Not me, of course. My parents had taken me to a magical therapist in New Orleans to have me checked out, and the verdict had come back "Magically Delayed." The magical healer had promised my parents I'd grow out of it, catch up to my peers, but it never happened. When I cast, my wand would either malfunction, as Big Jo's had done, or usually not do anything at all. When I was old enough to go to school, my parents decided to let me live as I was. After all, in the local elementary school, I was a normal kid. They never needed to cast any spells on me to keep my magic from showing itself. Kind of made it easy for everyone, in my opinion.

But now I was older, and, while I still didn't feel magic coursing through my body, there was the smallest tug from Big Jo's wand. Almost like my grandmother herself, who'd never accepted the healer's diagnosis, and would often try to goad my magic into making its appearance.

"Well, if I ask you to help me get the trash out, are you going to send me to another murder scene?" I asked the wand, as if it could respond.

Unsurprisingly, it didn't.

"Okay." I cracked my neck. "We can do this."

I tapped the bag nearest to me and willed it to rise. To my shock, it did so, and didn't catch on fire, turn into a lion, or some other alternative I couldn't even think of. It bounced and bobbed toward the open front door, and I followed it until it levitated and deposited itself into the larger dumpster.

"Well, I'll be." I looked at the wand, stunned. "All right then."

One by one, the trash bags closed themselves up and levitated out to the dumpster. Each time, I was sure something awful would happen, bracing myself for the other shoe to drop. My magic had *never* behaved so well.

"Last one," I said, lifting the wand and tapping it in the direction of the far-off trashcan.

And suddenly, I was bathed in darkness.

"I swear to the Fates, if there's another dead mermaid, I'm going to scream."

My eyes adjusted to the dim light, and my senses picked up on the sound lapping against the beach, the scent of the water, the feel of the night breeze on my cheeks. I reached into my pocket to grab my phone and turned on the flashlight, casting a glow along the beach.

No mermaids. But it definitely looked like I'd been transported right back to the murder scene.

"Great."

I went to walk toward the Cove, lit up in the distance, when my flashlight flickered on something white on the beach. I stopped, moving the light slowly across the sand until I saw it again. A card.

I knelt and flicked the sand away around it, careful not to touch the card itself. But I didn't need to do much before I recognized the logo, and the latter half of the email address.

Lewis Springer of the *Eldred's Hollow Caller*.

Chapter Thirteen

The right thing to do would've been to call up Vinnie, tell him I'd found a piece of evidence they'd missed at the crime scene, and go on my merry way. But as of right now, I didn't think Vinnie could be trusted. For all I knew, he'd chuck this into the trash, or say Lewis had probably dropped it while he was sniffing around that night, looking for the breaking news story. But something told me that this particular card had been in the possession of one dead mermaid, and that Lewis wasn't telling the whole truth about what he knew.

That night, I lay awake on the couch, replaying

that night over and over in my mind. Lewis couldn't have been the one to murder her, could he? What could he gain from it? No, it had to be something else. Maybe she was going to him to tell him something about someone, and that someone didn't want that to happen. Maybe it was all a coincidence.

Around two, I gave up trying to sleep and turned on mindless television (yay, internet) until I finally conked out.

However, at dawn, The Shack opened all the blinds and windows, letting in the light and ensuring I wouldn't be able to sleep in. I showered, dressed in another of Big Jo's shirts, and headed to the Enchanted Cat to discuss the latest with Kit and drink a gallon of coffee to wake up.

Only to find it closed.

Of course. It was Sunday. Nothing in Alabama was open Sunday morning except churches. And you wouldn't find any of those in Eldred's Hollow.

I spun on my heel, not terribly hungry but needing to find caffeine if I was going to deal with people all day. I got in my car to drive toward the non-magical town nearby—which would have a better chance of being open at this time of day—but a single broom parked in front of a building at the edge of town stopped me.

The *Eldred's Hollow Caller*.

"Hm."

The newsroom was a two-story building made of

red brick, with a large window out front bearing the newspaper's logo. I assumed Lewis lived in the apartment above, or it held offices like the Enchanted Cat, because the newspaper only took up the bottom floor. Lewis sat at a single desk, reading through a magazine. But all around him, pads and papers were scribbling, and photos were dripping on a line. I supposed magical ones didn't need darkness to develop.

I opened the door, and the bell above tinkled. Lewis jumped, reaching for his wand, as if he were expecting someone to hex him. I honestly kind of wished I could.

"Morning," I said with a smirk.

"Oh, Fates alive. Just you." He put his hand to his heart and released his grip on his wand. Then, as if remembering that I was a potential audience member, a cheesy smile curled onto his face. "Well, good morning to you, Little Jo. To what do I owe the pleasure? Here to compliment me on the latest edition of the Holl-Call?"

I hadn't read today's edition, but I'd seen the headlines the past couple of days. "Maria's murder seems to have fallen off the front page."

"So it has. Not much new on the matter." He shrugged. "Aimee's been arrested. The mermaid is dead. Until we get to court in a few months, there's nothing else really to discuss."

"That's funny," I said with a mirthless chuckle.

"Because I seem to remember your uncle milking my parents' deaths for weeks after it happened."

It had come out much meaner than I'd meant it to, as I was trying to play it cool.

Lewis's brows rose in surprise. "Well, now I understand the frosty reception last night."

"That, and you'd shoved a camera in my face ten minutes after I found a dead body," I said, crossing my arms over my chest. "So what gives with the lack of coverage? Have you had a change of heart? Decided that you aren't going to profit off the pain of others?"

"Maria wasn't a witch," he said, leaning back in his chair. "We really only cover witch business."

I quirked a brow. That was a load of bull if ever I'd heard one. "Then why was your card found near the crime scene?"

He stopped. "I'm sorry, what?"

I pulled the card from my pocket. "Found this last night in the same spot where Maria was murdered. Must've been covered up by sand, or the police weren't doing a great job of looking for clues. Either way." I tossed it down onto his desk. "Thought it was interesting you failed to mention that when we spoke the night she died."

"I'm sure this card fell out of someone's pocket." He was a terrible liar.

"Lewis, I may not have any magic, but I'm not an idiot," I said. "What were you talking with Maria about? Why would she have your card the night she died?"

"Well, as a *general* rule, I don't share what my sources tell me. But considering she's dead..." He leaned back in his chair. "Fine. We spoke a few hours before she died. It wasn't a *fruitful* conversation, so to speak. It was all I could do to get her to take my card."

"What did you talk about?"

He licked his lips, tapping his fingers on his desk and searching the room as if looking for an escape. "I *may* have heard that she was shopping around the idea of *perhaps* possibly, maybe in the future—"

"Spit it out."

"Selling a swath of property."

My eyebrows lifted. That certainly wasn't what I'd been expecting. "What kind of property does a mermaid own?"

"Well, obviously the entirety of the sound," he said, gesturing toward the south where the body of water lay. "But also a nice little stretch of beach a ways down the coastline. Can't get to it by roads, as it's basically swamp. Close to werewolf territory, though, which is probably why they were hassling her about it."

"Hassling her?" I took a step forward. "In what way?" I stopped. "Wait, was that what Carver wanted to talk about the night she died?"

He nodded. "I saw them leave together when I

got to the Cove and went to eavesdrop."

"Of course you did," I said with a roll of my eyes.

"Oh, come now," he said, as if anything he could say would improve my opinion of him. "We *do* have a happening gossip column that's been all over their on-again, off-again relationship. So I was hoping it might've been *on*, which would've been *such* a scandal, especially as everyone *knows* Natasha's trying to lock him down since he's going to be alpha—"

"Get on with it," I said. "What were they talking about?"

He shrugged. "I don't know, really. But I know Carver was offering her a large amount of money. She refused and told him to get lost. That's why they were arguing. Then he got in his car with Natasha and left, so I swooped in and—"

"Peppered her with questions," I finished for him. "I take it she didn't want to talk to you about it?"

"Not at all." He chuckled. "But I gave her my card in case she was feeling chatty later. My guess is Carver was there on behalf of Big Dog himself." His brown eyes sparkled. "So if *I* were going to be investigating, that's where I would go next."

"I'm not investigating," I said.

"Sure you aren't."

I glared at him. "Well, if I was confident Vinnie

was doing his job, I might leave well enough alone. As it stands, I feel like there's something else going on. Maybe you should write about *that* instead of gossip columns."

"Believe me, I will, once I get the full story," he said. "You know, you'd make a great reporter. I probably have a job here if—"

"Hard pass." I stopped, looking down at the card on his desk. "So Carver wasn't with her when she died, hm?"

"He was long gone when I spoke with her, around eight-thirty," Lewis said. "And before you ask, I *did* mention all this to Vinnie the night she died."

"Yet they still arrested Aimee," I said with a shake of my head.

"Well, there was a vial of mermaid-stunning potion near Maria's body. She did suffocate. It's not a stretch to think Aimee did it."

"Except she didn't," I snapped.

"I just go where the facts lead," he said with a shrug. "I suggest you do the same."

My mind whirling, I left the magical part of town and drove until I found a coffee shop that was open, where sucked down a quad-shot americano along with a hearty breakfast muffin. I grabbed another coffee to go and headed to the Cove, arriving five minutes before noon. The parking lot was already filling up, as were the marina and beach.

Aimee actually looked genuinely surprised to see me, and even more surprised when I plopped down a cup of coffee for her.

"What's this?"

"Coffee," I said.

"Oh." She made a face. "Hate the stuff."

I sighed. So much for a peace offering.

"Thank you for the thought, though," she said with a nudge. "And thank you for being here this morning. Looks like we've got a busy one ahead of us."

"Right." I snatched the other cup and took several long swigs. "What do you want me to do first, boss?"

She thumbed in the direction of the kitchen. "The kids we've got are pretty smart, so they don't need much oversight, but pop in every so often to make sure they're not letting orders sit too long." She nodded to the marina. "And I haven't been out there to collect yet, so you could start there."

"Will do."

She glanced at my right hand, where Big Jo's wand wasn't. "Did you use magic last night?"

"A bit," I said, deciding not to tell her about my second late-night excursion and the discovery of Lewis's card. "The wand seemed to know what to do."

"See?" She looked smug. "Now don't let me

catch you acting like you're not a witch. Clearly, it's in your blood."

I didn't feel like sticking around to argue, so I headed out to the marina to collect the cash from the boats tied up to the docks. On any given weekend, the Cove's marina was filled with boats of all kinds. About ten or so slips were rented out on a monthly basis to witches and other creatures who wanted to live the life on their boats. The other twenty were reserved for people out on an aquatic adventure. It was twenty dollars to dock for three hours, fifty for the whole day. If you didn't want to pay, you could always pull up on the beach, which was what most did after all the slips were taken.

I approached the first boat, which held a witch with a New England accent, who, by the looks of his red face, had forgotten that sunscreen existed.

"Yeah, glad to be here," he said, beaming at me from the deck of his boat. "Name's Pat Carrigan."

"Nice to meet you," I said, taking his money. "This is a nice boat."

"Not mine," he said with a laugh. "Rented it from the vamps across the way. Such a funny thing, vampires running a beach town. Kind of turns things on its head, don't you think?"

"Why'd you come here, then?" I asked. "Aren't there better places over on the other side of the sound?"

"Oh, sure. But you know, this place is

legendary," he said. "Gotta see where the witches party. Get a...what's it called? Witchwhacker?"

"That's the one," I said with a chuckle. "Make sure to pace yourself. They pack a punch."

"I'll keep that in mind," he said, stepping off the boat.

I watched him head toward the bar with a curious expression. Almost every boat here was from across the sound. It was possible that one or all of them had mermaid-stunning potion aboard. Maybe one of these rentals had brought it over?

"Hey, a question," I said after taking money from the next boat over. "What all comes with the boats they rent you?"

The warlock gave me a sideways look. "Hm?"

"Do they give you a kit, like something in case of emergencies?" I asked, glancing at the boat, hoping I might see it. Not that I thought I'd see the mermaid-stunning potion sitting around, but it didn't hurt to gawk.

"Oh, well, they gave us this kit in case we got in trouble," he said, nodding to a small box on the floor. "Flares, a potion to help with buoyancy if the boat sinks, that sort of thing."

"Anything to stun a mermaid?" I asked.

"Nah, they told us the mermaids don't bother the boaters," he said before concern fell on his face. "Is that not true? Should we be worried about mermaids?"

"Not at all," I said. "Enjoy the Cove. Try the burgers. They're fantastic."

Before long, every slip in the marina was taken, so those who motored up had to anchor out and walk ashore or pull up on the beach. I bounced around, listening for conversations that might give me more insight into Vinnie, Maria, and anything else going on in Eldred's Hollow, but everyone seemed to be from out of town. No one had any inkling a mermaid had died earlier in the week. Much like the other night, it made a familiar place seem unfamiliar, and I didn't like it.

With all the money collected from the boats, I headed back inside to check on the kitchen. As Aimee had said, a gaggle of teens were making food. There wasn't much to it, of course. Cooking hamburgers and hot dogs on the grill and tossing fries in the fryer, mostly, made easier with the magic most of them had. The kitchen had been where Kit and I had cut our teeth, once upon a time, and it made me a little happy to see the new crop of kids hard at work.

"How's it looking in here?" I asked, walking the line and checking receipts. Unlike a regular place, where the orders came in on paper receipts, here the words floated in the air, put out by the register at the front. The kids had to reach up every so often and pull the letters back down, or else they'd float away.

"Who are you?" one of the kids asked.

"This is Little Jo," said one of the other kids, who looked somewhat familiar.

I squinted at him for a moment before recognition dawned. "You're Harold Murphy's little brother, aren't you?"

He nodded. "Name's Sam."

The others rattled their names off, mostly witches and warlocks, but one—surprisingly enough—werewolf. I supposed Big Dog really was relaxing his opinions about intermingling with witches.

"We got a problem," Janelle said, walking out of the fridge with a few frozen patties. "We're really low on beef."

"Really? Who was supposed to order more?" I asked, looking at the kids suspiciously.

"I believe the person who was in charge of that died," Sam said without a lick of sarcasm.

Okay, he might've had a point there.

"Fine, I'll head to the grocery," I said. "You keep…well, keep doing what you're doing. I'll be back in a bit."

Chapter Fourteen

I could've sent one of the kids to get the meat, and they might've had an easier time of it with their perfectly functioning magic. But after talking with Lewis about Carver's offer to Maria, I wanted to see what I could get from the alpha himself.

Eldred's Hollow Grocery wasn't in the main town, but wasn't too far away, either. Grocery was a bit of a misnomer, as they were famous for the meat they bought from the farmers nearby. It wasn't the usual beef, pork, and chicken, either. They'd been known to get chimera meat, basilisk, and when possible, dragon. Their wild meats section was something impressive, too, but that was only stocked near the full moon, when the pack went hunting.

Big Dog Briggs (I hadn't a clue what his name actually was) had been the alpha of their pack since well before I was born. Werewolves didn't believe in monogamy, especially where their alpha was concerned, so lots of the wolves around here were somehow related to him. Carver wasn't his eldest son, but apparently, he had whatever he needed to surpass his other siblings and be in the running for alpha.

I'd always thought it bluster, but if Big Dog was giving him the stick, so to speak, to carry out deals on behalf of the alpha, maybe there was more weight to his standing than I'd anticipated.

Sadly, none of these questions were likely to get answered sitting here in the parking lot of the grocery store, so gathering my courage and confidence, I walked inside.

I was greeted by rows of normal-looking food products in familiar branding. A werewolf stood reading a magazine at the teller spot, popping her gum. She reminded me a bit of Daniel's assistant, and she very well could've been her sister or cousin.

"Oh, is that Little Jo?"

The booming, gravelly voice echoed across the store. I shouldn't have been surprised he'd scented me already.

"Come on back, kid! Let me get a good look at you."

I followed the sound of the voice until I reached the butcher counter in the back. Big Dog stood behind it wearing a white apron. To a normal human, he probably looked like any other middle-aged, over confident man with pale skin and medium-brown hair tucked into a hairnet. But to a witch, even one without magic like me, the power he exuded was almost indescribable. I wasn't sure if it was the werewolves who gave him that palpable feeling of "a man nobody's ever said no to" or if it was just his energy. He was way over six feet, with broad shoulders and thick muscles no man his age had any right to. As I approached, he watched me with a mix of pride and something almost predatory.

"Well, I'll be. You're all grown up, aren't you, Little Jo? How long has it been?"

"Eight...uh, eight years," I said, clearing my throat. Big Jo never acted like this around him, but she'd always been able to match his energy.

"So sorry about your grandmother. Loved her, you know? Pursued her a few years, too." He chuckled, and it was hard not to be grossed out by that. "But she loved her bar first and foremost. I take it you're going to be manning things from here on out? Moving back home?"

I cleared my throat. "Not at the moment. Just trying to tie up loose ends. Helping Aimee out today."

At the sound of the bartender's name, his expression darkened. "Absolutely outrageous what they're doing to her. As if Aimee could hurt a fly, let alone kill a mermaid. I told Martin—he's on the force you know—that they absolutely had the wrong person. He tells me they don't, and that they have, and I *quote*, indisputable evidence that she's responsible."

I couldn't believe he was telling me everything like this. "The vial, right?"

"But what witch *doesn't* have a vial that looks like that?" He chuckled, and I realized he must've thought the evidence they had against Aimee was any vial, not one with mermaid-stunning potion in it.

"I—" I began, but he was already on a roll.

"You witches and your potions. I have a few of them in my camper, too. You know, for aches and pains, plus the occasional romantic endeavor." He chuckled, his voice booming in the store and making me feel like I wanted to melt into the floor. "Still got the equipment, but these younger wolves, they like the *stamina*—"

"*Anyway*," I cleared my throat loudly, "I need to pick up some meat. Lots of folks at the marina today."

"Yeah, I was wondering when you'd come to get it," he said. "Big Jo always picked up her meat order on Thursdays," he said, tilting his head. "It's been sitting in the freezer for you. I figured you guys were probably running extra low."

"Yes, of course," I said with a bit of relief as he snapped his fingers to another werewolf behind the counter and pointed at me. "Thanks. Been a crazy week."

"Just a shame she passed before she was able to pass on what she knew," Big Dog said as the other werewolf threw large stacks of meat on the counter. "Carver doesn't want anything to do with this place, but if he wants to be considered for alpha, he's got to do more than swagger around here and pretend he's in charge. Leadership takes *intention*, you know? You have to *demand* respect from your people by showing you know what you're doing."

He was going off on another tangent, but the mention of Carver piqued my interest. "Yeah, I've seen him around the bar lately."

Big Dog let out a rather dog-like snort. "Pfft. He spends too much time there, and with his new girlfriend, if you ask me."

"Yeah, I heard she was related to you?" I asked. "How does that work?"

"She's the daughter of the brother of one of my mates," he said. "Not *blood* related to Carver, if that's what you're asking. We do have some standards here." He adjusted his apron as if it were a three-piece suit.

"Of course, of course." I cleared my throat. "They seem like a nice couple."

"Humph. I don't think she's a good match for him, but at least she's better than that mermaid." He grunted and rubbed his nose. "Not that I have anything against Maria, of course. Well, I didn't…"

Could Big Dog have been the one to…?

"Rest her soul," he added, almost as an afterthought. "I mean, I didn't like her for Carver. What future does he have with a fish girl, eh? But I liked *her* as a person. Always held her own with me. Never showed a lick of fear, even surrounded by the entire pack during the full moon."

Now *that* was impressive. Even walking into the grocery in broad daylight made me wary.

Big Dog seemed determined to hold this conversation with himself. I waited, hoping he might offer me a morsel of why he'd send Carver to offer her money for her land, but he didn't venture down that road.

"The sigh of relief I let out when she dumped him. He was tore up, of course. But he's a big dog. He'll move on." He paused. "Though he was devastated to find out that Maria was dead."

Devastated wasn't the word I would've used to describe Carver last night, but if I kept the conversation going, maybe Big Dog would give me something.

"The police say someone stunned her, dragged

her onto the beach, and left her there," I said. "Horrifying. Can't imagine why someone would want to hurt her."

"I can." He snorted. "Few weeks ago, I caught wind that *someone* was offering Maria a large sum of cash for a swath of swampland near our compound, and perhaps some of the sound."

That was easy. "Who?"

He gave me a look. "Who do you think's hanging around here with more cash that he can stuff his coffin with?"

I'd considered that, but I hadn't had definitive proof. "What does a vampire need with swampland?"

"Haven't a clue," he replied. "Probably bulldoze it and put up another high-rise hotel. He's snapping up all the land in the area he can get his undead little hands on. Heard Wilson Perry already sold to him and is leasing the land until Reaves is ready to use it."

I rubbed my chin. "So you sent Carver to, what? Give her a counteroffer?"

He nodded. "I'm not about to have some vampire put up a gaudy luxury hotel overlooking the compound, so I told Carver to make her an offer she couldn't refuse."

If Cal had offered me two million for the Cove, there was no telling what he'd offered Maria. The werewolves had money, but could they even compete with the mega-rich vampire? I suppose if the alternative was a high-rise, the werewolf would've pulled out all the stops to ensure it didn't happen.

"But she did refuse," I said with a slow nod. "Did she tell him why?"

"Probably because I sent a pup to do an alpha's job," he said gruffly. "I'd hoped, perhaps, she was level-headed enough to see beyond their past relationship. But if you talk to Carver, she was hysterical about him even coming near her. He said he couldn't get a word in edgewise because she told him to get out of her sight."

I swallowed my comment about unreliable narrators.

"In any case, two hours after he made the counteroffer, she showed up dead." He shook his head. "Can't say for sure if the timing is coincidental or not, but it sure smells fishy." He paused, chuckling. "No pun intended."

I nodded, needing to think. "Well, I should probably be getting back. I'm sure they've run out of meat by now, and there are hungry people waiting at the Cove."

"Don't want to keep them waiting, for sure." He winked then looked at the meat expectantly.

I stared at it, waiting.

"Aren't you going to do the," he waved his hand as if brandishing a wand, "thing?"

My face warmed. "Right. You probably don't remember, but—"

"Oh, still having trouble with the magic thing? No worries." He snapped his fingers, and that same young werewolf appeared from nowhere. "Do you have a car?"

I nodded.

"Consider it loaded."

When Big Dog said jump, the pups didn't even hesitate. Within minutes, my rental was laden with as much meat as we could fit, and I was on my way back to the Cove, my mind whirring.

Cal Reaves had always thrown his money around, but it had been limited to the other side of the sound. Now I knew of two people (myself included) he'd offered presumably large sums of money. I hadn't necessarily *felt* threatened when we'd spoken about it, but something about his offer raised the hair on the back of my neck.

I pulled into the Cove parking lot, intending to grab one of the kids to help me unload, but instead, my attention went to the crowd of people on the beach. I slammed the car door shut and jogged over, my pace increasing as the voice of one very irate mermaid duke echoed across the open air.

"*Bring me that woman!*"

I pushed through the crowd until I reached the shoreline, where I found Duke Pinfish, water shimmering on his bare chest, pointing a spear at the crowd gathered. Behind him, ten other mermaids, each wearing armor that looked made of coral, stood at attention with decidedly smaller spears. Luckily, Aimee was nowhere to be found, which was perhaps why he was bellowing at the crowd to bring her.

"What in the world is going on?" I barked, catching his attention.

The water rippled beneath him, pushing him onto shore to stand head and shoulders above me. I kept his stare with a confidence I certainly didn't feel, but I knew I couldn't break it.

"You witches are liars." His voice was unnecessarily loud, and I rubbed my ear.

"Take it down a notch, will you?" I said. "What could you possibly have to complain about? No mermaids have been seen at the Cove."

"Yes, but your disgusting vehicles have been doing zigzags over our home all day and night!" He gestured toward the marina. "And this morning, one of your *kind* used that *vile* potion on one of ours!" Another gesture with the pointy end of his spear toward the Cove. "Which means the time for *your* justice is over. I want *that* woman!"

"*That* woman is still innocent until proven otherwise," I reminded him. "And you're beholden to the rest of that council thing you were going on about, aren't you?"

His nostrils flared, making it clear he was only here because he'd gotten his fins in a twist, not because he had any jurisdiction to arrest her.

"As it stands, *we* don't use that potion here," I said. "My grandmother banned it from all the boats in her marina, and that ban is still in effect. So if someone brought it over, you should probably bother the fanged individuals on the other side of the sound."

"It's a witch's brew, therefore, a witch is responsible," he said, pointing his trident at me. "We're lucky the victim was already in the water and suffered no ill effects."

"Who was it?" I asked.

"No one you would know, witch," he replied. "But an innocent."

"Hardly!" Bobby Cutter stood on top of his fishing boat, which was in its slip, his hat askew as he pointed an irate finger at Pinfish. "These mermaids have been messing with our boats."

"Bobby," I said, trying to keep my calm. "Are you the one who used the potion?"

"No." He crossed his arms. "My boat's been in port all day."

"Then who was it?" I turned to the rest of those gathered, including the ones on the dock. "Speak up."

No one did.

"If I have to go boat to boat looking for the

potion, I will," I snapped. "And if I find any instance of that potion on my marina, that person's boat will be at the bottom of the sound, understand?"

"This...isn't my boat?" came the timid voice of the nearby captain. "Not that I used the...whatever it's called. But—"

I rubbed my temple. "Then *whoever it is* would forfeit their security deposit." I turned to Pinfish. "As for you, your mermaids are already forbidden from the Cove. We don't want any more trouble from you, nor are we trying to court any. Our law enforcement is working on finding a culprit for Maria's death. Be patient."

"I have very little patience. That woman is clearly the culprit," he said, his spear pointing toward the Cove again.

"I'm not so sure about that," I said. "Were you aware that Cal Reaves was trying to buy a large plot of land from Maria?"

Recognition flitted briefly across his face. "No."

"The werewolves gave her a counteroffer the night she died. Know anything about *that*?"

"What's your point?"

"The *point* is that it's *possible* someone killed Maria because she was or wasn't going to sell the land," I said. "It's called motive. Which is something Aimee doesn't have. So I suggest you stop threatening my employee."

"Or else what?" He lifted his chin higher, puffing out his bare chest. "You'll hex me?"

I didn't really have a response to that. "Would it be too much to ask for peace between our kind while we get to the bottom of this? I don't want to see anyone else get hurt." I nodded to the Cove in the distance. "I know you don't have any love for witches, but—"

"I owe *nothing* to you vile, land-dwelling creatures," he snapped, the water rising around him, making the boats in the marina rock. "And I would love nothing more than to see this entire place reclaimed by the sea."

Waves lapped higher, quickly overtaking my feet and rising to my ankles. The witches on the shore cried out in concern, brandishing their wands and running for higher ground. Pinfish watched them with glee.

I pulled my wand, knowing full well I *wasn't* going to use it but needing to do something to stop him.

"Knock it off." I pointed the wand at him. "I mean it."

Magic tingled down my arm, filling the wand. Something shot out, a spell, and within seconds, the merman and his entourage were gone. The water receded almost instantly, leaving me with wet shoes and a shocked feeling in my chest.

"W-what did you do?" a nearby warlock asked

me.

"I..." The answer rose up within me. "Banished them."

"You did?" Aimee stood behind me, her eyes wide with surprise. Where she'd come from, I hadn't a clue. "How'd you manage that?"

I stared at the wand. I had no idea.

Chapter Fifteen

"What kind of loose ends?"

The frustration in Joel's voice was unmistakable. It was Monday morning, and in the real world outside Eldred's Cove, it was time to get back to work. I'd been so consumed with mermaids and vampires and missing money that I'd actually *forgotten* what day it was until his number lit up my phone.

"Still working through the estate stuff," I said, watching The Shack redecorate itself. It had had the courtesy not to start until well after dawn, at least. Windows had been shifting along the walls for the past five minutes, and the front door had moved from one side of the place to the other. "And the lawyer suggested I stick around to manage the bar until we can figure out how it all shakes out."

"Bar?"

"Oh, right. Yeah. My grandmother owned a bar. Very popular down here." I ran my hand through my hair. Since it was a weekday, the Cove wouldn't open until later in the afternoon, so I had the day to run errands, including visiting the bank. "Anyway, I'm keeping tabs on email, and should be able to make meetings virtually."

"We really need you here, Jo. The client likes a hands-on touch, you know that. You won't be able to provide that from...where are you again?"

"Alabama," I said. "Small town between Mobile and Pensacola. You've probably never heard of it."

"Well, when do you think you'll be back?"

"Give me another week or two," I said, praying it wouldn't take longer than that.

We spoke in more detail about some outstanding issues, and at the end of the call, Joel seemed somewhat confident I wasn't disappearing into the ether and halfway placated about my impromptu two-week sabbatical.

"Hopefully, two weeks," I muttered to myself as I hung up. The envelope of money from the weekend was sitting on the counter, ready to be deposited. Next to it was Big Jo's wand.

I hadn't so much as touched it since placing it there the night before. Duke Pinfish and the mermaids hadn't shown up again, and even though I didn't know exactly *how* I'd banished them, I had a feeling it was only a Band-Aid. Duke Pinfish had a stormy temper, and the last thing a beach bar needed was to be on the bad side of a merman who controlled the water.

Although he was the biggest worry, the other revelations from the weekend hung heavily in my mind. Carver's offer to Maria the night she died. Cal's involvement in everything. Big Jo's mysterious missing money. I couldn't help but feel that if I could untangle *one* of these mysteries, the rest might reveal themselves, too.

Since I had to go to the bank anyway to deposit the cash, I figured that was a good place to start.

I left The Shack to its redecoration and headed to the Enchanted Cat Cafe for a coffee and a biscuit. Kit's dad was in the kitchen, frying up eggs and slinging hash. The front room was full but seemed back to its normal size.

"Hey, Jo," Kit said, appearing from the back with a fresh pot of coffee. "Sit anywhere you like. Hear you had a busy weekend."

"I'm sure you did." I took a seat at the end of the counter. "Coffee and biscuit, please."

"Dad, Jo wants two eggs, bacon, and grits," Kit said, winking at me. "You gotta regain your strength after doing all that spell work."

I glared at her. "Har har."

"So, you're now a full-fledged witch? What happened?" She put a mug in front of me and poured coffee into it.

"I'm not. It was one spell." I cleared my throat, picking up the coffee mug. "And it was a fluke. I didn't cast it. It just…cast itself."

"Spells don't cast themselves, Jo," Kit said, using her wand to float a plate full of pancakes to a table across the room.

"I don't know what to tell you." I leaned on the counter. "Because the spell certainly didn't come from me." In fact, none of the times the wand had worked seemed to have come from me. "This wand has a mind of its own, I guess. Like its former owner."

"Wands *also* don't do that," Kit said with a look. "But if you're casting, and it's not doing what you want, you should take it to the wand shop. The last thing you want is for the wand to cast the wrong spell when it counts."

I didn't have the heart to tell her it already had. But it wasn't a bad idea. The wand shop was next to the bank, so it would be easy to pop in afterward.

A plate of eggs, bacon, grits, and a biscuit landed next to me, not in front of me, but before I could ask Kit about it, Daniel sat and grabbed the sweet tea as it settled itself on the counter.

"Morning," he said.

"Morning," I replied, keeping my tone even. I still wasn't sure what to make of his friendship with Lewis, so I didn't want to give him anything that might end up in the newspapers tomorrow.

"I wanted to apologize again for barking at you on Saturday morning," he said, digging into his breakfast. "I don't remember the conversation at all."

"Seems odd that you don't," I said. "I mean, you're a lawyer. Shouldn't you be up at the crack of dawn or something?"

Kit, walking by, let out a snort of laughter. "Danny? Up at dawn?"

"Maybe if I don't go to sleep," he muttered.

"Well, don't come to The Shack, then," I replied. To his inquisitive look, I added, "Big Jo's house has been having a grand old time waking me up early the past few days. It doesn't like me very much." Kit put down my plate of breakfast food, and I snatched the biscuit with a pointed look. "Headed over to the bank. Gonna ask them about the mortgage."

"Why?" he asked. "They won't tell you anything without that death certificate."

"Daniel, this is *Eldred's Hollow*," I said with a hearty roll of my eyes. "I can't go anywhere without being recognized. If there's anywhere in the world I could get away with bending the rules, it's here."

"Sorry. Can't."

"What do you mean, you can't?" I scowled at the middle-aged witch across the bank counter from me. "You gladly took the money I gave you and deposited it."

"I can deposit funds, but until we get a legal document indicating you're the owner of the account, I can't help you." She lifted her glasses and stared at me like I was annoying her. "Is that all you needed today?"

"Is there a manager I can speak with?" I asked. "It's kind of important that we find out what's going on."

She sighed and tapped her wand against a piece of paper. A moment later, another middle-aged female witch appeared, this one wearing a smart suit and her graying hair in a bun. After a moment, I recognized her as the co-op owner's wife, Sherry.

"Little Jo!" She walked toward me with outstretched arms. "Tom said you were back in town. You're a sight, aren't you? Spitting image of your mother." She kept a firm grip on my shoulder. "Come on, let's go chat in my office."

The elder witch all but frog-marched me into her office and shut the door. She smiled at me as she sat at her desk and folded her hands together.

"How are you holding up?" she asked, tilting her head. "Things haven't been easy over there at the

Cove lately, have they?"

"You could say that again," I replied with a snort. "I was hoping you might be able to tell me some details about my grandmother's accounts. You know she took out a big mortgage on the Cove, right?"

Sherry nodded.

"Well, the money's gone," I said. "And neither Aimee nor I know what it was used for. Meanwhile, we've got this huge payment, and..." A pleading smile came to my lips. "Do you think you could help me figure out what's going on?"

"Do you have her death certificate?" Sherry asked.

"N-no, but—" I cleared my throat. "It's ordered. Daniel said it'll take a few weeks. But I figured, since you *know* who I am, and—"

She tutted and shook her head. "I really wish I could help. I do, honestly. But we were bought out by a larger bank two years ago. Bunch of kappas out of New Orleans own us now. They want *everything* done by the book." She shook her head. "They'd be on my broomstick like polish if they found out I was giving out information."

"But it's my information," I said. "I'm the only heir."

"And I know that. But they don't." She tilted her head again, pity on her face. "I hope you can understand that."

I did, in the non-magical world where people didn't know me from Lilith. But here, in Eldred's Hollow, where everyone seemed to know everything about my business whether I wanted them to or not, being told I couldn't access my grandmother's information without proper paperwork was startling.

"As soon as you get that death certificate, we'll start that process. I'll even get it going for you, fill out all the information you need." She stood, gesturing toward the door. "Goodness knows, I've got all of it."

"You can't even tell me where the money went?" I asked. "That's all I need to know, really. I'd like to recoup it so we can satisfy the mortgage. Or at least figure out what half a million dollars paid for."

"I'd be happy to tell you."

I brightened.

"As soon as you get the death certificate."

~

I supposed I could've stayed and argued more, but it seemed fruitless. I thought about calling Daniel to complain, but he'd probably tell me the same thing. There was nothing more to be done about the financial quagmire I'd inherited.

So the only thing *to* do was to walk inside the wand shop next door.

With all the magical creatures and ingredients being grown around Eldred's Hollow, it was no wonder the local wand shop bore a sign declaring they had the "freshest ingredients." Considering witches used the same wand for decades sometimes, I didn't see how "fresh" ingredients would make a wand better or worse. But everyone had to have a gimmick, I supposed.

The building was very similar to the others—brick, painted, large front window. But there was something whimsical about it, even from the outside. The awning that hung over the sidewalk seemed to dance in a non-existent breeze. Inside, the back wall was filled with tins bearing hand-scribbled labels describing their ingredients. On a back table, several cauldrons were bubbling, presumably with a unique concoction of ingredients to be used to enhance the wands' powers. Next to it, several wands still needing their potion and finishing polish sat ready to be doused.

"Hello?" I called, seeing no one. "Anyone here?"

The back curtain rustled, and Lois Boneham appeared. She had dark brown skin and black hair wound into tight braids that dangled down her back. "Good—oh!" She brightened. "Jo Maelstrom. How the heck are you?"

The Bonehams had been in Eldred's Hollow since before even my family had shown up and started the bar. Obviously, a town full of witches would need someone close to manufacture wands, and the plethora of wand-making ingredients added to the draw. Lois was a year or two older than me and would be the fifth Boneham to take on the mantle—or had already, perhaps, since I didn't see her mother.

"I'm good." I gestured around me. "What about you? Are you running this place now?"

"Please," she scoffed. "My mother's still the head honcho. But she has Mondays off, so she deigns to leave me in charge for a short period." She rolled her eyes affectionately. "I don't think she'll ever retire."

"I get it." I'd never thought Big Jo would retire either. Turned out I was right.

"What can I do for you?" she asked. "I hope… Maybe time to make you a new wand? I couldn't help but notice you didn't have one at the memorial."

I didn't have the heart to tell her I'd chucked it into the sound. Her mother had made it for me and had been one of the loudest voices egging Big Jo on to push me more. "Ah, no. Sorry. But I have been using Big Jo's wand a little, and I think it's malfunctioning."

"Impossible." She held out her hand.

I gave her the wand, and she inspected it like it was the inner workings of a computer. She tilted it this way and that, tossing it in the air and catching it, dangling it from her forefinger and thumb from the pointed end and the handle.

She placed it in a wand holder on the counter.

"No, it's working well. Quite active, that one. Is it one of ours?"

"I suppose so," I said. "She's had it as long as I can remember. So there's nothing wrong with it?"

"Not that I can tell," she said. "Which is a little puzzling in and of itself."

"Why?"

"Wands who've been with their wielder that long tend to form a bond, and many times the wand will cease to function when that witch or warlock dies. I've heard of some who've been working with very powerful witches for decades actually bursting into flames. But this..." She lifted a brow at me. "This one's very much alive, and if it's *working* for you, it seems to have recognized you as the owner."

"I wouldn't call it *working*," I said, rubbing the back of my head. "More like..."

She chuckled. "What's it doing when you use it?"

I felt ridiculous talking about the night Maria died, or the nights thereafter, but I did need to figure out what was going on. Lois listened intently, pursing her lips and furrowing her brow until I was done explaining the curiosities.

"You've always had trouble with magic, haven't you?" she said.

I nodded, my face burning. "I don't even know why I'm asking you about this. Clearly, the problem is me. It's always been me. I should just continue not using magic—"

"You're a witch, Jo. It's in your nature to want to wield," she said gently. "Obviously, witches have different levels of magic. And sometimes the right combination of ingredients in the finishing potion can bolster a lackluster amount of magic that another wand didn't recognize."

"I mean, I lost count of the number of potential wands they fitted me with," I said. "This one's producing something, just not the spell I intended."

"Mm." She ran her finger along the wand. "It's definitely reacting to something in your magic, that's for sure. Transportation spells are quite difficult to do. There's a reason most witches don't even attempt them when a broom will do fine. You're lucky that you've stayed in one piece doing them."

"I'm not trying to do them intentionally," I said, after a moment. "In fact, the last time it happened, I was trying to levitate the trash to go outside."

She continued inspecting the wand, touching it lovingly and watching it as if it were speaking to her, and giving up some great secret. "Let me ask my mom. This is a bit of a puzzler. Both the age of the wand, and that it decided to pick a new owner after decades with the old one." She lifted her finger. "Would you mind terribly if I kept it?"

Everything in me screamed to take it with me. "N-no. I don't—"

She lifted her hands in surrender. "Say no more. I know a bonded witch when I see one."

"Bonded?" I laughed nervously. "No, it's not like that."

"You looked at me like I was taking your left foot," she replied with a grin. "It's okay. Maybe you two need to get to know one another. It's so used to speaking in Big Jo's language that it's not understanding what you're saying, you know?"

I nodded slowly, and a little hope flared in my chest. "Do you think...maybe if we spent more time *talking*...I might be able to use it like a normal witch?"

She shrugged. "I can't tell you that. But there's no harm in practicing a little more."

There actually could be a lot *of harm.* I swallowed, pulling the wand back to me. "Thanks for the information. I really appreciate it."

"I'm still going to ask my mom about it. I know she's been dying for something to research lately that's not the latest combination of wand potion ingredients."

"I would've thought the best combinations would've been well-known by now..."

"Well, for the most part, sure," she said. "But with all the new technology, cars, Wi-Fi, cell service, satellites—all that can interfere with magic, you know? So they're always looking for something that might make magic work a little better in the modern era." She shrugged. "It's like adding grains of salt to a timer, in the grand scheme of things. But you know, she likes to stay busy."

I nodded.

"If I find out anything, I'll pop by the Cove," she said. "You're working there now, right?"

"For the moment," I said, looking down at the wand. "Thanks again for your help."

CHAPTER SIXTEEN

Practicing magic seemed like a dangerous thing to do, especially with a wand on the fritz, so I put Big Jo's wand in my back pocket as I headed to the Cove for the afternoon. There were a few cars in the parking lot already, and a couple of broomsticks in the holder, but it was otherwise quiet. Aimee was behind the bar, wiping it with a rag as Jimbo stared at her with his usual vacant expression.

"How's it going?" I asked, sliding onto a stool.

"Not great," she said. "Vinnie came by half an hour ago. He says they've...well, they've moved up the court date."

I frowned. "Why?"

"Apparently, Duke Pinfish has been pressuring the judge in New Orleans," she said with a thin expression. "Wants to get justice for Maria quickly. Especially since he's...uh, been *banished* from here."

"But...they don't have anything on you, right?" I asked.w "Just that vial, and that's not enough to convict anyone."

"Somehow, I feel like Pinfish is going to make sure the verdict comes back guilty," Aimee said. "He wants someone to blame. I'm an easy target."

"But you're innocent. Surely, he wants the *actual* culprit found, right?" I paused. "And if he doesn't, then why doesn't he?"

She shrugged. "Suppose that's yet another mystery to be solved."

"Look, why don't you head home?" I said. "I've been around here enough now to remember how it all works. Besides that, it's a Monday. Probably going to be a light crowd tonight. And you could probably use some rest."

"I'm not really supposed to work Mondays, but with Big Jo gone..." She let out a groan. "I can't leave. You can't manage the bar."

"Yes, I can," I said.

"Are you gonna pull out that wand and use it?" She put her hand on her hip. "Because you can't make a Witchwhacker without a little wand magic."

I pulled out Big Jo's wand, surveying it. Maybe

Lois was right. The wand and I needed to communicate with each other more. After all, it had made a million Witchwhackers over its lifespan with Big Jo. Maybe it would understand the task.

I whispered a small prayer to the Fates that I didn't end up in Mobile, then tapped my wand against the glass. To my—and Aimee's—surprise, the liquid changed color.

"Well, I'll be." She picked up the drink and downed it. "Look at that. Could've come from Big Jo herself."

I couldn't help the beam of pride.

"Well, if you've got things here," she said. "I would like to pay Daniel a visit before he gets off for the day. Ask him what I should do or..." She shivered. "What I need to prepare myself for in case they manage to convict me."

She hopped on her broom and flew off, and I watched her go with more than a little anger. Something wasn't adding up. Nobody seemed to be looking for the real culprit, but they were real keen to pin this on the first person they could find. That meant either someone had something to hide, or someone was taking advantage of the situation.

Either way, it wasn't fair to Aimee.

I considered all I knew about Maria's last few days so far. The vamps and the werewolves had offered her a large sum of money to sell off a piece of swampland for who knew what purpose. As much as it would've made sense, motive-wise, for another mermaid to kill Maria, they wouldn't have used the potion on their own kind. Which meant it was someone on land.

The vamps, of course, were plausible. Cal Reaves was snapping up property as fast as he could—and if Maria was planning on selling to someone else, maybe he thought he'd have better luck with a different mermaid. But Duke Pinfish seemed to have no love for anyone up here.

The werewolves were still suspicious, too. How far would Big Dog have gone to protect his compound? If he'd caught wind of Maria thinking of selling, maybe he'd wanted to prevent the deal from happening. Maybe after talking with Carver, Big Dog had sent another werewolf to finish the job so his son would have an ironclad alibi.

Or was there some other suspect, some other motive I hadn't yet uncovered?

Five o'clock arrived, and with it, an influx of people eager for their after-work drink before heading home. The Eldred's Hollow ferry had been stopping at the marina dock all day with a smattering of passengers, but the last one was practically overflowing with witches and warlocks getting off from a day at the hotels.

Aimee's daughter Grace was among them. She walked into the bar, her brow furrowing. "Where's my mom?"

"Sent her home," I said. "I can handle things for the evening."

"Are you sure?" She glanced at the wand sitting next to my hand. "Are you able to use that thing?"

I had made no fewer than ten Witchwhackers in the hour since Aimee had left, and the wand hadn't misfired once. I was starting to really lean into the theory that the wand was so used to the spell that it had no trouble remembering how to do it. It certainly didn't make the *rest* of magical living easier, but if I could do this one thing, then the next week or so would be. At least Aimee wouldn't have to work seven days a week.

Grace perched at the bar, watching me pour drinks and talk to customers, getting a Witchwhacker for herself and tasting it to make sure it was up to her standards. I didn't take offense—I'd be suspicious myself—but I was somewhat relieved when she stood and nodded at me.

"I'm headed home. Got an early morning." She pulled on her jacket. "You seem to have this handled."

"If I don't, I'll be sure to let you know," I said.

She walked outside, hopped on her broom, and floated down the street.

"Well, goodness me. Aren't you a sight?" Stuart, one of the many who'd departed the ferry, stood in front of the bar with a smile on his face. "If I wasn't wearing my glasses, I'd swear you were your grandmother, slinging drinks and tending bar like a pro."

"Now that's a compliment if ever I've heard one." I leaned on the bar. "Want a drink? Dinner?"

He ordered a beer, but declined food, citing his new rule that he was only eating bar food on Friday nights. "I'm not getting any younger. Need to keep myself fit for the long haul."

"I get you." I handed him the bottle. "You know, if I do decide to stick around, I might try to improve the food offerings. Something not fried might be a refreshing change."

He took a long sip. "Are you considering it?"

I honestly wasn't sure. Before, when I'd assumed I was useless at magic, the thought of staying was ridiculous. But the past hour had felt good, and perhaps it was the salt air messing with my brain, but I'd started to think managing this place might not be so ridiculous after all.

"Who knows?" I said, after a long pause. "My boss in Atlanta sure wants me back."

"You'd be better off going back, if you ask me." He made a face. "Seas have been rough since Duke Pinfish got his tail in a twist. Used to be only a hurricane would give us three- or four-foot waves in the sound. Now it's all I can do to keep the ferry afloat going back and forth."

I'd noticed the whitecaps out in the sound but hadn't connected it to Pinfish. "He's certainly positioned himself as judge, jury, and executioner. Aimee said they were moving up her trial date to next month. They seem to think they have a slam dunk."

"Or the money to make it one," he said.

I gave him a sideways look. "You think something weird's going on, too, don't you?"

"Something weird's always going on, especially where a lot of money's concerned." He finished off his beer, leaving the bottle on the bar. "That's why I think you should leave. This place is a gem, but I'm worried Maria's not the only one who's gonna end up on the wrong side of the water. It would kill me if anything happened to you, Little Jo." His wet eyes crinkled as he smiled. "You're all I got left of your grandmother."

I patted his hand. "Don't worry. I've got a temperamental wand and a bar with a huge mortgage I can barely cover. What could go wrong?"

The night wore on slowly but steadily, with the usuals coming for their after-dinner drink and leaving shortly thereafter. By seven, there were only a few stragglers in the place, and by eight, it was me, my work laptop, and Jimbo, who was perched in his usual spot, staring at me and begging for scraps.

"Sorry, bird," I said, eyeing him as I worked through emails that had come in during my shift. Since, of course, there was no internet here, I had to use my phone as a hotspot. Luckily, there was great service. "No leftovers for you. Kitchen's closed."

He let out a *haa* and clapped his beak angrily.

"Complain all you want," I replied, reading another email a few times so I understood what they were asking for. "Maybe you could go catch a fish or a crab or something. You know, like a real seagull."

He flapped down to stand beside me and opened his beak wide to let out a loud *Ha ha ha* in my ear then flew away. I rubbed the side of my head, glaring at his retreating tail feathers, before returning to my laptop.

Even though I'd worked earlier in the day, the number of undone tasks was steadily growing, and there would surely be more tomorrow. A nagging little voice in my mind told me that very soon, I'd need to choose: stay here in Eldred's Hollow and work the Cove until I figured out Big Jo's issues, or leave it all behind and return to the real world of websites, data, and ornery clients.

At eight-thirty, I rose from the stool and stretched. Would the wand help me clean up or would do something insane again?

"Okay." I cracked my neck. "Nice and easy. Let's see about putting all the chairs on top of the table, eh? Just like Big Jo used to ask of you."

I tapped the first chair, and the legs sprang to life, bending as if it were a ballet dancer. Then, with a small *whee!* the chair flipped onto its head on the table.

"Cool." I wasn't going to take anything for granted. "Now the next one."

It might've been faster to do it manually, but I wanted the practice. Needed it, almost. Wanted to prove to myself that the drink-making wasn't a fluke, that I could ease my way into the business of the bar. Even if I planned to leave it all behind again, some part of my inner child needed to know they still belonged.

As the chairs did their flips, I walked to the rolled-up walls that came down to secure the place and protect it from the elements. With a nervous breath, I tapped the first roll, and it came tumbling down, as expected. Then, like a cascade, the rest followed suit, until the entire room was enclosed by firm, see-through walls.

"Well, thank you," I said to the wand. "That certainly made everything a lot easier."

The last time I'd tried to take out the trash magically, I'd ended up at the crime scene again. I decided to do it manually. There weren't that many, as it had been a quiet night, and the task was completed within minutes.

I stood at the bar and scanned, looking for anything amiss or any tasks I'd forgotten. Everything looked locked up and ready for tomorrow's fun. The only thing left to do was count the money and check receipts, which Big Jo always left for last.

I opened the register and pulled the cash drawer, taking it with me into the office. Jimbo cried as he followed me into the office, sitting on his perch to watch me.

"Still don't have any food for you," I said, counting the bills, starting with the largest. "Did you wrestle up dinner?"

Ha.

"I don't know if that's a yes or a no," I said, grabbing the next stack and counting them quickly. "But if you want to come with me, I haven't eaten, so I was going to head into the regular part of town and get some drive-thru."

Ha!

"That's right, you don't leave here." I paused and looked at him. "Fine, I'll swing by on my way home. French fries?"

Ha! Ha! Ha!

"Aren't familiars supposed to communicate with words?" I muttered, grabbing the ones and working my way through them first. When I finished, I tallied up the numbers I'd scribbled down. It didn't seem like a lot. And when I flipped back to last week's numbers for the same day, I frowned. We'd made double last week what we had today. One day could've been an aberration, but between this weekend's receipts and today, I was sensing a downward trend that was certainly going to run afoul of our large mortgage payment due at the end of the month. For the millionth time, I checked in file cabinets and under folders and everywhere I could think of in search of *some* hint about this money and where it might've gone to, since the bank managers weren't being very helpful.

"You weren't going senile, were you, Big Jo?" I muttered, hoping she hadn't become the victim of an internet scam of some kind. That was the last thing I needed.

"Hello?"

I grabbed Big Jo's wand and I walked out into the front room, relaxing when I found Karen standing by the front door.

"Hey!" I said. "Sorry, I closed up for the night. But I could probably get you a beer if you wanted?"

"I have kids, remember?" She laughed. "I got them to bed and wanted to stop by to tell you I'd found your potion-maker."

I jolted, having almost completely forgotten I'd asked her to look into that for me. "You did?"

She reached into her pocket and handed me a scrap of paper with a name on it. "I asked around about where one might find a mermaid-stunning potion. You'd have thought I was asking people to give up their firstborn child."

"It is frowned upon," I said.

"Frowned upon and widely used," she said. "But finally, I got a name. Nobody local. It's a witch out of Charleston. The vamps commissioned her to make the potion, and they get it shipped in. Tell the tourists and the mermaids it keeps barnacles off. But really, they've got it plastered all over their charter boats going into the Gulf."

"If the vamps are the ones who keep handing this stuff out, how did a vial end up here?" I asked. "And more importantly, why are we being blamed for it?"

"That I can't answer," she said. "This wasn't super easy information to find, I will say. They aren't broadcasting that they've got this stuff on every boat they're renting out."

"If they aren't broadcasting it, how do the renters know what it is?" I asked.

"Well, that's the sneaky part," Karen said. "The potion they've concocted isn't like a regular one. It's oil-based. So they coat the hulls of their rental boats with it and when it dries, it still maintains its properties. The boat can sail through the water, no problem. But if a mermaid touches the hull—boom!"

That certainly explained Duke Pinfish showing up irate the other day. "How long does the effect last?"

"Who knows? The only thing my friend at the rental dock would tell me was what I told you—and he told me I couldn't breathe a word of it to anyone with fins, or he'd be out of a job."

"Not as if we're having a lot of conversations

with finned folk at the moment," I said with a sigh. "Guess that means I'm headed to the beach in the morning."

"Good luck," she said with a smile. "Let me know if I can do anything else."

Chapter Seventeen

The next morning, bright and early, I stood with a gaggle of other commuters and a few tourists, waiting for the ferry. The sound was, if possible, rougher than the day before, with high whitecaps that seemed out of place without any wind to push them. Duke Pinfish was keen to make life miserable for anyone who wanted to use his waters until he had justice for Maria.

Possibly due to the rough waters, the ferry was late, and Stuart was all apologies, but he looked happy to see me, at least.

"You're up bright and early," he said. "Beach

day?"

"Thought I'd check it out," I said, not wanting to share the true details of my trip with anyone. "Been a while."

"I'd steer clear of the water, if I were you." He thumbed toward the high waves. "It's even worse on the Gulf side. Red flags all over the place. Nobody's swimming, which is a darn shame. But the merfolk do what they want."

For a split second, I reconsidered taking the ferry across, not wanting Pinfish to rise out of the water and take his revenge on me—along with a boatload of other people—but Stuart, seeming to read my mind, gave me a wink.

"Don't you worry. I've got wards on this ship out the wazoo. Nobody's gonna be tipping us over any time soon. I can't promise a smooth ride, but we'll get you there in one piece."

He wasn't kidding. The ride over was horrific. I'd never been one to get seasick, but I was certainly green by the time the ferry sidled up on the other side. The rest of the passengers were wobbly as they exited the boat, some of them having to empty their stomachs off the dock before continuing to the city.

"I did my best," Stuart said to me as I was the last one to leave. "But these mermaids are steaming mad, you know?"

"Well, if you happen to see one of them, please let them know I'm not interested in keeping this war going," I said. "Aimee's innocent, but *if* they want to work together to find the real culprit, I'd be happy to tell them what I know."

He pushed his hat up. "You know something?"

"Well, not yet." I stared at the high-rises and picture-perfect streets beyond. "But I will."

"Good luck." He turned to walk back onto the ferry but stopped. "If you ask me, you should go get some fried oysters from the Oyster Pearl. It's inside the Grand Gulf Hotel." He winked. "Not that I want to make any enemies on the other side of the sound, but they've got the best ones, in my humble opinion."

"I'll be sure to do that." I smiled. "Thanks, Stuart. I'll see you in a few hours."

Big Jo had told me that when she'd moved to Eldred's Hollow as a little girl, the beach across the sound was nothing but a flat barrier island, covered in white sand, sticker bushes, and sea oats that kept the dunes from washing away in storms. Now, the sidewalks beneath my feet were pristine, the grass an almost unnatural green. Even the sun seemed to shine brighter over here, but perhaps that was because it was reflected by the glass-covered buildings. Fountains and other water features sat in front of the large, gated condos and hotels that stretched up into the crystal blue sky. Every car had an out-of-town license plate, and every face on the street was somewhat sunburned.

The good news was, since it was a tourist town now, there were helpful maps plastered on light posts every other block. I stopped in front of one, searching for anything that might indicate a watercraft rental place. I assumed Cal owned everything on this island now, including the recreations, so I headed in the direction of the first one I found.

On the sound-side of one of the "smaller" buildings (in that it was only twenty stories instead of thirty) was a long stretch of beach covered in all kinds of boats. Kayaks, canoes, jet skis, and the motorboats that came to the Cove every so often. I hadn't really noticed that they were all the same, but lined up like this, the shared coloring and branding was impossible to miss.

A young witch was working behind the counter, staring at her phone as I walked up. She put it down, glancing around as if looking for her boss to come scold her for goofing off on the job, before finally turning to me. Thankfully, she didn't seem to recognize me at all. The benefit of crossing a body of water, I guessed.

"Morning," she said. "What do you want to rent?"

"Oh, um." I turned to the shoreline, realizing at that moment I hadn't come up with a plan. "I guess I was curious about the safety measures you guys had. I've had some bad experiences with mermaids in the past. I hear you guys have some clans around here."

"Ummm... I don't know." And based on her vacant expression, she probably didn't. "I can ask my manager, though."

Seemed like something a salesperson should've known, but I nodded and let her disappear behind the open door. I didn't actually want to talk to her manager, as there was a better chance they might recognize me or send me away for asking questions. But I was close enough to that back door, I thought...maybe if I could summon?

It was a big ask. While Big Jo's wand had undoubtedly summoned a lot, the last time I'd tried it, the results had been disastrous. But after all day yesterday without a mishap, I was feeling oddly confident.

"Okay," I whispered to the wand. "Bring me the mermaid-stunning potion."

I waved the wand and closed my eyes, magic shimmering down my arm into the wand and giving me hope that maybe, *maybe*, I'd finally figured this magic thing out. But when I opened my eyes, there wasn't a potion vial in my hand.

In fact, my hand wasn't there at all.

"What the—" No, not my hand. My arm. My feet. My legs. When I touched my stomach and legs, they were physically there. But when I looked down, it was sand and water.

I'd somehow turned myself invisible.

"Just frickin' perfect." I ran my hand over my hair, grateful to feel the strands under my fingertips, at least. How I'd managed to do this, I hadn't a clue, but I was sure if I asked Lois, she'd tell me it was some complex spell only advanced witches attempted. Or that she'd tell me I was stuck this way for the rest of my life.

Either way, I—

"Well? Where is she?"

I jumped at the angry voice as a vampire came storming out of the small shack, his white-blonde hair slicked back and his linen suit way too fine for a man who (presumably) managed a watercraft rental service. His red-faced subordinate was behind him, squeezing her hands together as she frantically looked around.

I started, ready to run, then remembered that *they couldn't see me.*

"She was right here," the poor witch mumbled, looking like she'd already been lectured for interrupting him. "Guess she didn't want to wait."

He let out a frustrated sigh. "Michelle, what did I tell you to say when people asked about mermaids?"

"Um..." Her face grew bright red. "I don't remember."

"Mermaids *are not* a problem in Eldred's Beach," he said, enunciating every word as if she were a small child. "Understand? That is the line we tell customers."

"But…" She rubbed her arms.

"In fact, tell them we don't have them in the sound." He gestured to the water beyond. "Nothing to worry about."

I straightened. *That* was a lie.

"But there are mermaids in the sound, I thought?" she said. "I mean, I've seen them—"

He gave her a look like he was regretting his teenaged hire. "We've added precautions so they won't bother our customers. So as far as they're concerned, there aren't any mermaids here."

Precautions. Would mermaid-stunning potions be a part of that?

"Then why don't we tell them that?"

Fates bless her, she really had no clue.

"Because it's a delicate situation," he said, clearly trying to choose his words wisely. "Now, tell me again: what do we do when someone asks about mermaids?"

"They aren't here," she recited, almost robotically. "The sound is safe for watercraft of all kinds. There's no need to worry. Give me your money."

He glared at her for that last comment but said nothing more and disappeared back into his cave.

The teenager stuck her tongue out at him and returned to her stool, pulling out her phone and watching videos I could vaguely hear. I stood motionless for a second, before slowly walking toward her. She was too engrossed in her phone to notice the footprints on the white sand, but the creak in the wood was unmistakable.

I winced, watching her, but she didn't look up, swiping on her phone to watch another video.

I kept moving, tiptoeing through the door the vamp had gone through. It wasn't enough that he'd alluded to his precautions. I needed the actual potion.

And also for the police to believe me, but I'd cross that bridge when I came to it.

The vampire manager had taken great pains to block out any sunlight so he could move about freely. But I didn't actually *see* him. I kept walking, conscious of the sound of my feet on the ground, until I found a door—and on the other side of that, a downward staircase.

That wasn't creepy or anything.

Holding my breath, I descended the stairs, hoping I wouldn't run into anyone. I was invisible, but I still had a presence, and if someone were to brush up against me, they'd surely feel it. I didn't see the manager at all, though, until I reached the bottom of the stairs. He was sitting in an office, watching some soap opera and sucking down a glass of blood. I was grateful the invisibility magic hid my disgusted expression.

The door on the other side of the room was open, and I was able to slip through without making a sound.

It took a minute to understand what I was looking at. A long, narrow road made of gravel lined with shops stretched out before me. The sound of rushing water echoed through the cavern, which stretched up into the darkness overhead.

The vampires had built themselves a whole town under Eldred's Beach?

I shouldn't have been surprised, and yet, I was mesmerized by everything. The beach flooded every time there was even a tropical storm, yet they'd managed to put this whole thing together and keep it intact—but then, even my limited magic picked up on the tingle in the air. Another partnership between witch and vampire.

I let my gaze wander as I strolled down the narrow street. Each shop was its own building with a narrow alley between them, and they seemed to lack for none of the modern conveniences tailored for the vampire audience. There were shops carrying blood-based treats, dark wardrobes with SPF 100, and even—ugh—*coffins*. One store seemed a bit more *magical* than the others, and the woman inside was, in fact, a witch.

I didn't have to wait long before a vamp came by to open the door, and as soon as she was through, I slid in behind her. The witch at the counter brightened, standing under one of those seasonal affective disorder heat lamps.

"Good morning," she said. "What can I do for you today?"

"Just this." The vamp picked up one of the many large tins sitting on a table in the center of the shop. Upon closer inspection, they showed an SPF amount and a promise to keep the evil sun off delicate skin.

Vampire makeup. So that was where Cal got his stuff.

While the vampire chatted with the witch, I did a quick scan of the store. Not that I thought there would be mermaid-stunning potion down here, out in the open, but maybe in the back? I didn't want to get too close to the witch, lest she sense me—and my escape was leaving.

But as I tried to slip out with her, I bumped into her in my haste, and she spun around, looking at me as if she could see me.

After a moment, she shook herself and continued down the street.

I put my hand to my head, telling myself I needed to be more careful, when I saw a familiar face inside one of the large-windowed shops.

Cal Reaves was getting yet another white linen suit fitted. The tailor hovered around his feet, adjusting the hem and pulling it down, speaking up to him with an adoration that seemed borderline obsessive. I stood in front of the window pressed my ear against it to try to hear their conversation.

"Yes, this is a fine fit," Cal said, admiring the sleeves.

"Doused in the finest witch's brew for keeping the sun off one's skin," the tailor replied. "Do you like it, sir?"

"I do, indeed. Fine work, James."

The tailor flashed a grin, confirming that he, too, was a vamp.

Cal stepped into a dressing room, and a few moments later, returned in a smart black suit without a tie, heading for the door without another word to the tailor.

I sprang back from the window, intent on following him. But Cal stopped in the middle of the narrow street, looking over his shoulder. I could've sworn he was looking directly at me, but his dark eyes never focused on my exact spot. He sniffed, an uncharacteristic sneer on his face, and turned back to continue walking.

I was keeping my distance, making sure to avoid vampires on the street, when there was a tingle in my fingers. I lifted my hand and actually *saw* a faint outline. *Fates.* It was probably a good thing I wasn't going to be invisible forever, but the dang spell could've waited until I was out of vampire land before turning me back.

But no, I was at forty percent opacity now, if I

were to guess, and since a witch appearing in the street out of nowhere might cause a stir, I dashed back into the safety of an alleyway until I was fully formed. I peered out, searching for any sign of Cal, but the streets were clear.

"Well, Jo Maelstrom."

I jumped nearly out of my skin, spinning around to where Cal was standing ten feet behind me.

"H-hey, Cal," I said, struggling to look like I wasn't scared out of my mind. "Fancy seeing you here."

"In the vampire underground?" he asked with a quirked brow. "It's more interesting seeing *you* here."

"Oh. Um." I scanned the street, desperate for something that might give me a good excuse to be here. I didn't think it was illegal for a witch to be wandering the streets, but as I didn't work here, there wasn't a good reason for me to be down here. Finally, my gaze landed on a shop selling tinctures of blood. "Aimee sent me here to get a fresh pint of blood. Y-you know, in case we get a vampire looking for a drink."

He smiled, and for a brief, terrifying moment, I thought he might've caught me in my lie. "You'll probably want more than a pint. Vampires can be a thirsty bunch."

I let out a nervous laugh, inching backward.

"Well, I've got enough arms for a pint, so—"

"Why don't I arrange for a full fridge to be sent to the Cove?" he said, coming to stand beside me in a single, fluid movement. I didn't even feel the air move. "It's the least I can do, especially with your dear grandmother passing so suddenly."

"That would be...lovely," I said, uncomfortable with how close he was to me.

"Excellent. Now that's out of the way, why don't you pop by for a drink more palatable to your witch sensibilities?" I didn't think he'd take no for an answer. "Come, come, my offices are right up ahead."

Chapter Eighteen

I supposed any other owner of a massive hotel chain would live in the penthouse, but Cal Reaves lived in the basement—for obvious reasons. I was a little nervous to be going to his private residences. After all, the vamp wouldn't just...kill me down here, would he?

To be safe, I fired off a text to Kit telling her where I was. But, of course, there wasn't much of a signal, so it stalled out.

"Can I get you a drink?" Cal asked. To my disgusted face, he added, "I have the full gamut of options for my non-vampire guests. Whatever your heart desires, I can provide."

As we walked into the expansive (and dark) living room, a butler appeared. Based on his pallor, he was also a vampire—or maybe he lacked any coloring because he worked underground.

"A water, then, for my guest," Cal said to the man.

He sprang into action as if electrocuted and walked to a large bar area on the other side of the room.

I took in the rest of the space: expensive-looking modern art on the walls, a sculpture of a naked woman in the corner, white leather couches in the center of the room, complete with a fire pit that surely never got turned on in the Alabama heat. Cal led me to the couches, and as soon as I sat, his butler returned with a glass and bottle of sparkling water imported from Europe on a black platter and bowed slightly as he offered them to me. When I took them, he looked back at me with dead, soulless eyes.

"T-thank you," I said, taken aback.

"This is my familiar, Dietrich," Cal said, waving to the man as he returned to the bar once more. "Are you educated on vampire familiars?"

"Not in the least."

"A familiar is a human bonded to a vampire master for the rest of their mortal life," he said.

"Willingly?" I asked, glancing at the soulless-eyed man behind the bar.

"Of course," Cal said, slathering on that southern drawl enough that I knew he was bending the truth. "Dietrich was a poor, orphaned boy when I came across him in Germany. The war had taken his parents, and he was on the verge of starvation. I practically saved him."

I frowned. "Which war?"

"The great one." He paused. "I believe you call it World War One these days." He chuckled. "There've been so many human wars in my lifetime, I've lost count."

"So you found this guy in what? 1920?" He was old, for sure, but he looked about sixty, not over a hundred.

"In exchange for their service, familiars get extended life," Cal said, as if reading my mind. "Not immortal, like me, but an extra thirty years or so. Not to mention the luxury of living as a vampire does, with all the trappings of wealth one could ask for."

And being their mindless slave. Didn't sound like the kind of life I wanted.

"Alas, Dietrich will probably be the last familiar I take," Cal continued, as the man brought him a glass of dark red liquid that could only be blood. "The practice has lost favor in the past twenty years or so. A familiar used to be essential to a vampire living and thriving in the modern world. They could go out in the day and fetch what we needed, that sort of thing. But now, of course, with the witchy potions y'all brew," he gestured to the makeup covering his face, "it's less necessary."

Dietrich showed no sign of hearing his master.

"So why not release him?" I asked.

"Dietrich's been mine for so long that he's of little use elsewhere," Cal said, beaming at his familiar as if he were a favorite dog. "An unfortunate side effect of the vampire-familiar bond is that the human's brain gets a little...muddled. I doubt Dietrich could even care for himself without my suggestions to do so." He sighed. "But, in time, he will pass away like the rest of my familiars have, and when he does, I won't take another."

This whole conversation was giving me the creeps, so I adjusted myself on the couch and took a hesitant sip of the very expensive water. "So what did you want to talk about?"

He smiled, revealing his fangs. "Surely, you know. The Cove! I wanted to ask if you'd changed your mind about selling it to me. Especially based on recent events."

"Such as?"

"Duke Pinfish has all but declared war on the place. I'm sure that's not helping you pay that large mortgage your grandmother took out." He tilted his head. "Am I wrong?"

"You aren't wrong, but I'm curious where you're

getting all this information from," I said.

"Witches talk. I employ witches at my hotels. I hear things." He shrugged. "It's nothing nefarious. But I confess, I've had my eye on the Cove for a long time. Your grandmother would tell you I'd been trying to get her to sell to me for at least twenty years."

"She never mentioned it," I said.

"From what I understand, you two weren't really talking."

"You do hear things." I took another sip so I wouldn't say something rude. After all, I was underground, and I didn't see any staircase to get back to the sun. Did vampire hotels have to meet building codes?

"I'm sorry. That wasn't very nice," he said. "It's probably a sore subject."

"You know, you're not the only one who hears things," I said. "I heard you were trying to buy property from Maria. Apparently, you were in a bidding war with Big Dog."

He snorted. "The werewolves think they can keep up with me. But if she'd entertained their offer, I'd simply have doubled mine."

"Why are you so keen on a piece of swampland?" I asked.

He beamed. "Well, because I have a vision."

As if summoned by telepathy, (which he probably was), Dietrich appeared next to Cal with a large binder that he gently placed in front of me, titled *Eldred Beach Resort and Golf Course Vision*. Cal crossed his legs, took a sip of blood, and nodded at the binder for me to open it.

I opened the first page and was greeted with a mockup of a golf course with homes strategically clustered around the place. At first, it looked like somewhere else, but I quickly recognized the curve of the coastline and the inlets. This was his vision for Eldred's Hollow—a ritzy, glamorous, sprawling, unrecognizable…thing.

"Are you…serious?" I looked up at him.

"Very." He uncrossed his legs and leaned toward me. "Over in Florida, they've taken what was a patch of barren, sand-spur-covered land and turned it into a multi-million-dollar resort and conference center. No such thing exists for the supernatural crowd. Imagine if we could host a witch's convention or a werewolf commune at a state-of-the-art center instead of…well, wherever they do it now."

"I don't think there are witch's conventions," I said with a thin smile. My gaze raked across the coastline until I found where the Cove was—and was relieved to find it still there.

"I meant what I said. I would keep the Cove, perhaps with a few minor upgrades to appeal to the higher-end clientele I plan to attract."

I put my hand on the cluster of homes that was

where The Shack and my parents' log cabin currently stood, tamping down something angry by reminding myself that the land was still mine.

"And my property? You'd turn it into, what? A subdivision?"

"Oh, don't be crass." He chuckled. "It would be a combination of rental properties and homes. Some people would own them outright and live there. Others would use them as vacation properties. From what I gather over in Destin, it's quite a mix of people."

Mix of people. Somehow I doubted anyone currently living in Eldred's Hollow would've been able to afford to live in their own town anymore.

"I know it seems drastic, but this is the future," he said, sounding unnaturally soft and sincere. "Progress can't be stopped, as much as others try. I've been on this earth a long time, and the ones who end up the best for it are the ones who stand aside and make their claim early." He smiled at me. "Everyone who's sold to me so far has been *very* well compensated. And I'm willing to go higher on the figure I quoted you."

I looked at the map again, seeing that some plots had been colored green. There were still more than a few holdouts, but there was more green than I liked. Farming, even magical farming, was hard work. I could see why they'd want to take the money and run.

Something on the east caught my eye. A bridge connecting Eldred's Hollow to Eldred's Beach.

"What's this?" I asked.

"Ah, well, that's one of the biggest pipe dreams," he said. "It's such a bear to get from the Hollow to the Beach, isn't it? Quite inefficient."

I pursed my lips. "Take the ferry."

"A ferry." He waved me off. "Pfft. Slow and obsolete. Can't tell you the number of times that boat's broken down over the past year. Who wants to travel on some predetermined schedule, at the mercy of the whims of the mechanics?"

"Everyone who's ever taken public transport." I did it all the time in Atlanta. "You want to build a bridge?"

"Obviously, it would take some effort. Having to get approval from the mermaids is the first hurdle." He tilted his head and pointed to the spot where the bridge met Eldred's Hollow. "That's what I was trying to buy from Maria. That and the strip of underwater land that would connect the beaches."

I bit my lip. Big Dog was right to be suspicious.

"As I told you, I hear things from the witches and warlocks who work for me," he said. "And they're *dying* for a faster route—especially one that wouldn't require a ferry ticket every day. Goodness knows that sort of cost can add up. With this bridge, they'd be able to zip across in twenty minutes. Not to mention all the tourists from the Beach can get to all the places in the Hollow. Think of your dear friend's Enchanted Cat Cafe, suddenly busier than they know what to do with!"

"Assuming all those witches and warlocks still live in the Hollow," I said, pointing to the clusters of homes. "Because your plan would kick them out."

He flashed me another fanged smile. "Nobody's kicking anyone out, as I said. I'm a very fair man. I want to ensure that everyone who does business with me is well compensated. I wouldn't dream of moving forward with anything until I had the full buy-in of the local community."

Or, he'd have bought up so much land that the holdouts would have no choice but to sell or be lost in the mix.

"So, now you've seen my vision." Cal sat back, crossing his legs with a fanged smile. "Are you ready to sell to me?"

"Did Maria know about this vision?" I asked. "All of it? Or that you wanted her land?"

"She did." He nodded. "We were very close to an agreement before her untimely death. It has certainly set things back for me, but not irretrievably so. As soon as a new clan leader has been chosen by Duke Pinfish, I plan on presenting them the same offer."

"Do you think they'll take it?" I asked.

He shrugged. "I can't see why they wouldn't.

Maria had plenty of opinions on safeguards for her people, and I gladly made sure each and every one was accounted for." He tilted his head. "She was quite thorough. A true leader. She will certainly be missed."

"Duke Pinfish seems to have taken over for the moment," I said. "At least, he's the one who keeps coming up to the Cove to complain about things."

He chuckled. "He's a different sort, that's for sure. I believe he's less used to interacting with witches and other magical creatures. In the Gulf of Mexico, his domain is far removed from most everything." He cracked a smile. "I confess that I've got a bit of an advantage with him in that I'm *not* a witch. So far, I've managed to stay far enough away from the current quagmire between your kind and his that we're still on good terms."

"Have you met with him?" I asked.

"Here and there," he said, a little evasively.

"And is he going to sell the swampland to you?" I asked.

"Ah." He chuckled. "I can't comment on pending deals. But rest assured." He flashed me another smile. "I always get what I want. The benefit of immortality."

I held my breath, not sure I wanted to ask the question but unable to help myself. "And does Pinfish know you're coating your recreation boats with the same mermaid-stunning potion that killed

Maria?"

He smiled. "I don't believe there's a single boat in the sound or Gulf that doesn't have that potion smeared on its hull."

"I can think of a few," I said. "I don't think the ferry—"

He quirked a brow.

"Stuart doesn't use it," I said emphatically.

"You should ask him on your way back." He smiled and rose, and I got the sense he wanted to end this conversation before it continued down that road. "I doubt Duke Pinfish will begrudge me for protecting my investments. Boats are expensive, you know. Can't have them ending up at the bottom of the sound."

"I suppose not." Pinfish would probably say there shouldn't *be* any boats in his sound, but I didn't want to voice that.

"You will give some more thought to my offer, yes?"

"I will, I promise." I paused, realizing I had a ready-made excuse to put him off a bit longer. "You know, I can't do anything until I get her estate squared away, which requires a few steps before I can even start that process. The bank won't even let me see her accounts right now."

"I understand how tricky the banks can be, believe me." Dietrich was at the door, his soulless eyes staring blankly ahead. "When you are able to make a decision, I hope you'll consider my offer."

"I certainly will."

Dietrich helped me get back to surface level via a well-hidden elevator, and once I stepped off, it snapped closed, and he was gone. I stood in the center of the posh hotel, brightly lit by the floor-to-ceiling windows that gave an almost panoramic view of the Gulf of Mexico. All around me, tourists of all supernatural stripes were coming and going, wearing either bathing suits and towels or brightly colored vacation clothes. There was a faint smell of chlorine in the air, and the temperature felt a little too clammy for the spring day outside. It certainly seemed a different world from Eldred's Hollow.

I walked back to the ferry, thinking about what the Hollow might look like under Cal's vision. The families who'd been there for generations wouldn't be there anymore, and all the regulars who hopped off the ferry and came to the Cove wouldn't be passing through either. Everyone would disperse, and the rural, quiet town of witches and magical creatures would turn into something I didn't recognize.

But was that a bad thing?

I waited an hour for the ferry to take me back to Eldred's Cove, as I'd missed it. It gave me a lot of time to think more about Cal's vision—and what he'd told me about the potion. I didn't believe for a second that *every* boat in the sound had it. My grandmother had brokered that truce with Maria's predecessors and been adamant about keeping her end of the bargain. But she only controlled the boats permanently docked in her marina, and Fates knew we didn't have time to check every boat that docked for the day during the busy season.

The better question was how had the vamps gotten away with it for so long?

"Short trip today, eh, Jo?" Stuart asked as I boarded the ferry,

"You said it." I paused, looking at him. "Stuart... Do you use mermaid-stunning potion on the hull of your boat?"

He frowned, taking a step back. "Why do you ask?"

"Something Cal Reaves said to me," I replied. "That there wasn't a boat in the harbor that didn't have it. Is that true?"

"Don't be getting me in trouble with anyone, Jo," he said, nervous laughter bubbling from his throat. "It's...not uncommon. The mermaids can get feisty, especially any that come in from the Gulf. Better to be prepared, you know?" He paused. "Why are you interested?"

I sighed. "Just trying to figure out what else I don't know about this place."

"You were so young when you left," Stuart said. "I'm sure there are a lot of things you thought you knew as a kid."

I thought about Stuart's business in the face of a new bridge connecting the beach and the Hollow. Who'd want to wait for a ferry if they could drive (or broomstick) across? Did he have any idea what was coming his way?

"What is it?" he asked, tilting his head at me.

"Nothing," I replied with a fake smile and kept walking.

Chapter Nineteen

The trip back seemed slower than the one there, and even though the ship rocked and turned in the frothy waves, I couldn't help but watch the shoreline where Cal's bridge would be built—a thick mess of pine trees and swampland.

For the first time, I thought about what Maria might've done with a few million dollars. Mermaids paid for drinks and food on land, but did they have a thriving economy below the water? Would Maria have taken the money and gone somewhere else with it? Did mermaids retire on beaches?

Somehow, I got the impression the money

wasn't the important thing. From what Cal had said, she seemed more interested in improving the lives of the sea creatures in the sound. If that were the case, she'd have better luck *not* selling.

Could Cal have killed her in an attempt to circumvent her? Would Duke Pinfish be more amenable to selling since he didn't live in the sound? What could Cal offer the Duke that would make him jump?

All the witches gone. That wasn't exactly what the vamp was proposing, but it was pretty close. I doubted all those vacation homes and rentals would be taken by witches and warlocks. There was a whole world of supernatural out there, if the past week was any indication, and the witches who'd made Eldred's Hollow what it was would certainly be pushed out.

I didn't have a good answer, but the whole conversation left a decidedly icky feeling in my chest.

An hour later, the ferry docked. There were still a few hours until the Cove opened, so I got in my car and drove through town, no destination in mind. I wanted to compare the old storefronts of Eldred's Hollow to the shiny, new buildings across the sound. Everything in the Hollow looked like it could've used a fresh coat of paint, but that was part of the charm, wasn't it?

I stopped at the light, my gaze turning to the

Enchanted Cat Cafe. If Cal got his way, would Kit and her parents sell their place? Would Daniel give up his office? Where would they go? Where would Lois and her mother at the wand shop go? Where would they get their fresh ingredients for making wand potions if all the farmland turned into a golf course?

For that matter, where would all the animals go? Surely, there were more farmlands that specialized in unicorns and dragons, but...

I sighed as the light turned green and kept driving until I'd circled back to the Cove. There, I sat for a moment, gazing at the empty parking lot and trying to envision this place under vampire ownership. But the idea made me so itchy that I had to put it out of my mind. The Cove was a witch bar, and as long as I made decisions about it, it would remain that way.

Inside, Aimee was already behind the bar, restocking liquor bottles. She barely acknowledged me as I walked up to her.

"How'd I do?" I asked with a hopeful smile.

She didn't look up. "With what?"

"Cleaning up?"

She stopped and looked around. "Oh, that's right. You did lock up last night." She took a step back, as if the thought hadn't even occurred to her, then continued what she was doing.

"That good, huh?" I said, sitting down on a stool

across from her.

She ducked beneath the bar. "I have a lot on my mind."

"That's true," I said. "Receipts were down again last night."

"They're going to be down until we make peace with the mermaids," she said, nodding to the sound. "Haven't a clue how we're going to do that, but we need to."

"Well, maybe we make peace by turning their ire on someone else," I said. "I found out who else is using the potion. The vamps. Apparently, every boat in their employ has it plastered on their hull."

"That seems…" She shook her head. "Are you sure?"

"I went to vamp beach today to find out for myself," I said. "Ran into Cal Reaves, who confirmed it." I paused. "Did you know there was a whole town under Eldred Beach?"

"Haven't been there myself, but yes." She cracked a smile. "How'd you end up down there?"

"Long story." I'd rather not tell her about becoming invisible, though I was sure she'd get a kick out of my misfortune. "But I ran into Cal, he invited me over for a drink and to keep pressing me to sell. Told me about his *vision* for the Hollow."

She frowned. "Which was?"

"A fancy, hoity-toity resort and golf course," I replied. "Lots of expensive vacation homes, condos, and hotels. He wants to make it a real supernatural vacation spot, one where he can host conferences and events and all manner of things. Which is fine, if he wants to keep all that on the other side of the sound. But he's got a whole new map of Eldred's Hollow and it's practically unrecognizable."

Aimee clicked her tongue. "I wonder if the farmers who sold him their land knew what he has in store for it?"

"Who knows," I replied. "He made it seem like everyone went into these deals with eyes open, but even in our short conversation, he seemed like he was twisting the truth. Said he wasn't going to touch the Cove if I sold it to him, but we all know that's a lie."

She eyed me. "You aren't considering it—"

"Not at the moment, no," I said. "Even less now that I know what he plans to do with it. But...I wonder how far Cal would go to get what he wants."

"What do you mean?"

"He said he was in negotiations with Maria to sell him a piece of property near here. He's planning on putting in a *bridge*, if you can believe it."

"A bridge?" She turned away, confusion on her face. "Where's he gonna put a bridge around here?"

"The swamp near the werewolves," I said.

"Big Dog won't be happy about that," Aimee muttered with a shudder. "Nobody would be. Can you imagine the noise? The traffic? All so the tourists can get from the interstate to Cal's hotels faster."

"The night she was killed, Big Dog sent Carver to counter Cal's offer," I said with a look. "So either one of them could've killed Maria."

"Goodness, you have been busy," Aimee said. "Are you a detective now or something?"

"Honestly, I'm trying to clear your name," I said. "But now… Well, I can't say I'm not a *little* worried for my own safety. If the wolves or Cal are willing to kill a mermaid to get what they want, what's to say they won't do the same thing to me?"

"First off, we don't know it was them," Aimee said, placing a reassuring hand on my arm. "After all, if you ask Vinnie, I did it."

I snorted, and she flashed me a wry smile. "There's another angle to all this, too," I said, ticking off my fingers. "First Big Jo dies, then the mermaid shows up dead, with the Cove's manager as the prime suspect. The mermaids, who make up a large part of our income, stop showing up. We have this big mortgage to pay." I gestured to the Cove. "It's not a stretch to think someone's trying to make selling more attractive."

"That's a big leap," Aimee said. "Cal's capable of a lot, as is Big Dog, but I don't think they'd go that far. No matter how much they want the other side to lose. Despite how they swagger around, they're both civilized men. They'll get what they want by throwing money around."

I probably knew the answer, but it was worth asking, "Did you know about any of this? Do you think Big Jo did?"

"If she did, she kept it close to the vest," Aimee said. "She seemed preoccupied before her death, but I hadn't imagined all this. A *bridge*? Buying up the entire town to turn it into a golf course and resort?" She filled the ice bucket with her wand. "But I can't imagine anyone wanting to hurt Maria over it."

"She was preoccupied?" I asked. Aimee hadn't mentioned that before.

"I mean, looking back on it, in the context of all we know now, yeah." She turned to me, resting her hand on the rag. "I hadn't thought too much about it at the time. Then I was too busy getting arrested for a crime I didn't commit. But... She seemed off. More than usual. She even mentioned how heartbroken she was that you hadn't called her back in several weeks."

"Ouch." I hadn't really wanted to go there.

Aimee gave me a look. "Did you two have a tiff or something? Why'd you stop taking her calls?"

"It wasn't so much stop, as...never start," I said.

"Why?"

I'd told myself that she reminded me of all my failures growing up, and every conversation would bring those memories to the surface. But sitting here, in her bar, I understood the real reason for my distance. I hadn't thought I was strong enough to endure another goodbye. So, I'd kept her at arm's length, so much so that her death barely registered on my emotions.

Mission accomplished, I supposed.

"No use thinking about it now," I said, my voice a little thick with emotion. "I'm here now, despite my boss yelling at me via emails. And I'm not leaving until we clear your name."

Aimee gave me an affirming smile. "I have to say, I'm glad you're on my side, Jo."

I couldn't help but notice the lack of "little."
"Me, too."

Five o'clock rolled around, and the bar filled with commuters. I was chattier than I had been, talking up regulars and dancing around the subject of Cal's plan, the mermaid-stunning potion, and anything else that might bring me closer to finding Maria's killer. But most everyone was only interested in shooting the breeze, talking about the latest college football recruit, and comparing notes on the latest potions or wand combinations.

As the sun cast an orange glow on the water, the charter boats and fishing vessels came in. I considered asking them if they had the stunning potion on board. How would I know if they were lying? Could I check their hulls? Was there a spell I could cast? Assuming Big Jo's wand would cooperate.

Billy Carver glared at me as he walked off the dock, perhaps sensing that I was looking at him. If anyone could've killed a mermaid, it was probably that ornery old bat.

"Are you gonna do something about the water out there?" he snapped at me. "I about tipped over five times today."

"What do you want *me* to do?" I asked, shrugging.

"You and the mermaids keep going back and forth," he said, gesturing to the sound. "That merking is taking his fury out on the rest of us."

"I'm pretty sure he's a duke, not a king," I said. "And he's the one being unreasonable, not me. If he'd quit threatening my bartender, I'd be happy to talk with him."

"Good." Billy sneered. "Because there he is."

My stomach dropped as the already-disturbed water rippled. The telltale sign of shadows creeping up toward the Cove were barely visible in the dwindling light.

Aimee and I shared a look of concern, and I put up my hand. "You stay here." I hurried around the bar. "I'll handle this."

As I approached the beach, Pinfish emerged from the water with his merry band, all holding their spears and coral armor and looking quite fearsome.

Pinfish looked past me toward the Cove, pointing his spear and bellowing, "Bring me that witch!"

"Glad to see you found a way around my banishment spell," I said, though I was pretty sure those things wore off after a while. At least, the people Big Jo had banished always ended up coming back the next day.

"My patience has run out," he said. "We're here for the murderer."

"Then please tell me you've gotten some actual evidence," I said, crossing my arms.

He flashed a mirthless smile. "The council in New Orleans has granted me permission to mete out justice myself. We will take her to the Aquatic Council and deal with her there. Whatever 'evidence' you want to present, you'll have to bring to her trial."

And figure out a way to get to the bottom of the Gulf, too.

"I don't think so." I met his gaze with a confidence I didn't feel. "Aimee isn't responsible for Maria's death. You've got the wrong person."

"Then who is the *right* person?" Duke asked, the water moving him closer to land but not quite on it.

I stood my ground, not wanting to show any weakness by stepping back. My gaze landed somewhere near his navel, and I had to crane my neck to meet his eyes. "Our local police force is on the job," I said with a smile. "I'm sure they'll have an answer for you quite soon."

"We've conducted our own investigation," he said, pointing his spear toward the Cove. "And we've determined it's *that* witch who took one of our own."

"Really?" I cocked my head. "What witnesses have you spoken to? Because I've been conducting a little search of my own, and I found out that the vampires across the way are the ones coating their boats in mermaid-stunning potion. Maybe you should go bother Cal Reaves."

He stared me down, and to my surprise, backed up. "You will hand her over or we will start sinking boats," he said, jabbing a finger in my direction. "Do you understand?"

Almost instantly, the boats began rocking, banging loudly into the posts in the dock. Billy Cutter, who'd slunk back to his boat to finish up for the day, cried out in surprise as he fell over.

"Give me a few days," I said. Then, because the boats were still crashing into the dock, I added an emphatic, "Please. I want to find the real culprit as much as you do."

He surveyed me, his eyes softening a hair. "You have until week's end. Three days."

With that, he dove into the water, his shadow disappearing into the depths of the sound. I didn't exhale until it was completely gone.

"Three days, that's great," I muttered, putting my hand to my head as I walked back to the Cove. "Three days."

"He's really going to take me down there, isn't he?" Aimee said as I passed her.

"Not if I have anything to say about it," I said.

"Jo, what in the world can you do that hasn't already been done?" she whispered.

I hadn't a clue. But I wasn't going to give up until I figured out what had really happened.

Chapter Twenty

Even though we couldn't afford it, we closed early. Most of the customers had watched the back-and-forth with Duke Pinfish, and none of them seemed eager to get in the middle of our fight. But those who were still hanging around got the boot, first from me, then, much more firmly, from Aimee.

When the customers were gone, it was Aimee's turn to get the boot. She protested, but I told her I didn't want her near any bodies of water, in case the mermaids got impatient. In the end, she got on her broomstick and left with explicit instructions to text when she arrived home safely.

After her broom disappeared, I turned to the marina, checking in with each of the captains to make sure their vessels hadn't been too badly damaged by Pinfish's watery threat. The sound looked to be much calmer than it had in days. Perhaps Pinfish had really taken my plea to heart and was giving me a break.

"We're all good here," said Jimmy Westwood, who ran a charter boat for tourists. "But I gotta tell you, Little Jo, I'm a little nervous about leaving my boat here overnight. What if the mermaids come back? It's about to be summer. I can't be without a boat."

The unsaid request was clear. "If you want to move to safer harbors for a bit, I'll prorate your rent."

Another thing I didn't have the funds to do, but he had a point. Part of the promise of a slip was relatively safe waters, something I could no longer guarantee.

In the end, everyone opted to dock elsewhere. Probably across the sound at the many open slots Cal Reaves offered. It was more money leaving my hands—money that we desperately needed—but better that than being sued for their damaged vessels.

I returned to the Cove and tapped each of the plastic walls to drop them, which would tell any potential customers that we were closed for business.

I tapped the chairs, and they walked themselves on top of the table. I even managed to bewitch a rag to wipe the counter while I went to count money in the office.

We hadn't made much. Maybe fifty dollars for the whole evening—which would be wiped out by the money I owed the boat captains. Jimbo flew in to cry at me, and I waved him away, not in the mood to deal with his tantrums about not getting french fries. He flapped his wings over my head, *ha ha ha*-ing, and I pointed Big Jo's wand at him.

"Go elsewhere," I snapped.

He gave me as dirty a look as a seagull could then flew away. I honestly didn't care if he was gone for good. I didn't see how he was of any benefit to me.

With the receipts counted and the cash in the envelope, I wearily walked to my rental car, making a mental note that I needed to extend it again. Some part of me whispered that I should fly back to Atlanta and get my own vehicle, but that would be admitting that I would be here indefinitely.

A glutton for punishment, I checked my emails. One included a calendar invite from my boss to discuss my current situation. Also, I'd missed a meeting with a client earlier that day.

Great.

I put my phone aside and headed back to The Shack, hoping for a good, long shower and no tricks from the sentient house.

The Shack was, for once, inviting as I wearily walked through the front door. There was a chair waiting for me, and I slumped into it, the weight of the day and the world falling on me at once. I rubbed my face in my hands, sitting still as the chair slid across the wooden floor to return me to the kitchen. A mug of tea came tumbling toward me next, and for once, I didn't decline, sipping eagerly and trusting that The Shack knew when things were dire. The tea was delicious and lifted my spirits a hair, which was to say that I no longer felt like curling into a ball and dissolving into nothing.

I stared at the ceiling, wishing I could walk upstairs and talk with my grandmother. In the darkest days after my parents died, when I couldn't be comforted by anything, having her near, knowing she was upstairs, at least allowed me to sleep at night. Now, the whole place was as empty as my mood.

"What are we going to do?" I said to no one.

Aimee had only a few days left to prove her innocence. I hadn't a clue where to go from here. The mystery person Maria had been meeting with could've been Carver or Cal or someone else—and there wasn't even any proof they were the one who'd killed her. The vampires had mermaid-stunning potion, but then again, so did everyone else. Big Jo's rule seemed like a joke, lip service paid to the clan leader to keep them from sinking boats. Carver, of course, had a rock solid alibi and witnesses.

Once again, I cursed the gift of magic for all it *didn't* do. I pulled Big Jo's wand from its hiding spot and stared at it. A magical wand that could only make drinks and close up a restaurant was great for someone who managed the Cove, but for solving the mystery of the mermaid's death? Terrible.

I twirled it in my hands, somehow sensing that it wanted me to give it more credit. It *had* performed some complex spells without my asking or knowing how, such as transporting me right to Maria's body. And later, when I'd found Lewis's card at the crime scene. Turning invisible had been mortifying, but...

"But it did lead me to the vampire underground, and Cal," I muttered, holding the wand steady for a moment.

Maybe it wasn't being so random after all.

I might not have agreed with the methods, but I couldn't argue that the wand was putting me exactly where I needed to go. And if Lois was to be believed, it was manifesting complex and dangerous spells without a second thought. I didn't even want to know how hard turning invisible was, but I hadn't seen any mention of it in my limited magical studies, so I put it on par with the transportation spells.

I sat up from the slouch I'd been in and held the

wand out in front of me. It was, admittedly, dangerous for me to try complex spells again. There really was no telling if *this* time, the magic would split me in half or any of the other horrible things that Lois had warned me about. But I was getting desperate, and I seemed to be the only one who could help Aimee.

"I need to find something that will exonerate Aimee," I said with a breath.

Then I waved the wand and closed my eyes.

Magic poured through me, chilling me from the feet up.

No.

My feet were wet.

I opened my eyes to absolute darkness, looking down at the swamp beneath my feet. The wand was still in my hand, but I could barely see it, let alone anything else. The moon was hidden behind a thick blanket of clouds, and the only light seemed to be from the condos twinkling across the water.

"Why am I here?" I whispered to no one, stuffing the wand back in its hiding spot and trudging forward. The muck squelched beneath my feet, and I could only imagine what I was wading through. And with. Alabama wasn't at a loss for creepy crawlies in our waterways.

"Please, no snakes," I muttered, walking forward. "Nice water moccasins. Leave me alone, please…"

I stopped in my tracks as voices echoed through the darkness. I turned in a circle, looking for the source, and found two shadows a bit farther down the path.

"...planning to sell this land to me."

My breath hitched. *Cal Reaves?* But who was he...

Even before Duke Pinfish spoke, I recognized the vortex of water and the large torso. "I highly doubt that."

"There's so much to be gained from selling this land, you know. A bridge connecting the Hollow and the Beach would mean—"

"More trash, more oil in my ocean, more vibrations to scare away our fish and make life unbearable for us." Pinfish puffed out his chest. "Is that the sort of thing you're after?"

"Not at all," Cal said, his voice practically oozing charm. "But with that much money, surely the local mermaid clan could relocate somewhere else. Perhaps the Gulf clan would welcome them."

Pinfish growled menacingly, and I almost feared for the vampire's life, except he was on solid ground.

"We aren't relocating from our ancestral lands to appease vampires. It's bad enough we have to hide from the regular humans."

Cal seemed to have recognized his misstep, and I was somewhat relieved that the vampire wasn't completely perfect all the time. "Of course, of course. But I wonder if Maria shared my *vision* for the future of Eldred's Hollow with you?"

Pinfish gestured toward him to continue.

"I've purchased about forty percent of the farmland here, hoping to get another large parcel in the next few weeks. Once I've amassed eighty percent, I plan on breaking ground on the construction of a state-of-the-art resort and golf course."

"I fail to see how that interests me."

"Well, this new resort would cater to a *specific* clientele. And all the witches who currently inhabit this area, perhaps the werewolves, too, would be..." He gestured. "Somewhere else. With total control over this area, I would be able to enforce certain restrictions on where and how people interact with your oceans. No more nonstop motorboats ruining your evenings, or trash floating down into your bay."

"Can you guarantee that?" he asked with a curious look.

"Have you seen a single piece of trash come off my boat rentals?" he asked. "The witches I do have in my employ have cast all manner of charms and wards to keep the trash inside the boats. And they're working on a way to magic their boats so they run on potions, not gasoline. Really, Duke Pinfish, my *vision* is all of us living more harmoniously. Merfolk and land dwellers, able to coexist without stepping on each other's..." He chuckled. "Tails."

Pinfish was silent, and I desperately wanted to know what was going through his mind.

"Maria and I were in final negotiations," he said. "She'd made me adhere to every single one of her demands, which included the concerns you've identified, and I intend to keep them."

Pinfish finally spoke. "You aren't the only one interested in that parcel of land, you know. The werewolves, for one, had offered quite a large sum. And the witch that Maria was meeting with before her death was bringing an offer of a million dollars."

I started. She was meeting with another witch? Who in town had a million dollars lying around?

Big Jo's mortgage. Could Big Jo have been working with someone who had continued on after her death? And if so...who? And why hadn't they come forward yet?

I could probably answer that last one.

"A million?" Cal scoffed. "My offer to her was well north of four million. An offer I'm happy to extend to you, as well."

"The only thing that would part me from this land is your promise that that disgusting cesspool of a bar would be wiped from the map," Pinfish said.

I glared at him, especially as Cal smiled. "Well, I can almost guarantee that. That young Jo Maelstrom will be selling her property any day now. There's quite a large debt, and with all the bad PR they've been getting lately, I'm sure that the pressure's on to satisfy the mortgage by selling it. Besides that, I can't imagine a witch without magic would want to stick around a magical town for very long. She visited me the other day and seemed almost ready to sign."

A lie! I wasn't even remotely close to signing. Also, I very much took offense to a vampire telling the mermaid I didn't have magic. I could make a Witchwhacker and close up shop, thank you very much.

"What would you do with the Cove?" Pinfish asked, rubbing his chin as if the idea were more interesting to him than the millions of dollars Cal was promising.

"Bulldoze it with the rest of the witch's lands," he said. "The golf course is going to take at least 2,400 acres, so we'll need all the space we can get. Besides that, no one paying $400 a night to stay at our resorts will want to go to some dive bar with sticky floors and no walls. They'll expect luxury, and that's what we will provide."

The floors weren't *sticky*. Sandy, perhaps. But not sticky.

"I say, I might like to see that," Pinfish said with a look. "Those nasty witches and their stunning potions. Had three mermaids go down this past week from it. I'd be happy if a witch never set foot on the beach here again."

"I can make sure of that."

I stomped my feet in anger. How dare that vamp stand there and let Pinfish accuse witches of stunning his mermaids, when he was doing it, too?

"Do I hear a change in the winds?" Cal continued. "Are you thinking you might accept my offer?"

Pinfish chuckled. "I'm considering it, but I haven't quite decided yet. I'll be in touch."

The funnel of water carried him into the sound, then all was quiet. Cal stood there for a few more minutes, perhaps waiting for the shadow of the mermaid to fully disappear under the moonlight before he took out his phone.

"Dietrich."

A moment later, a speedboat that had probably cost more than my first car came zooming up the water, helmed by none other than Cal's elderly familiar. The nose of the boat pushed against the soft sand, and Cal stepped into the water to board the boat. Immediately, the familiar proffered a pair of new shoes, taking the wet ones from his master and putting them away.

"Well, Dietrich, I think we might be closer than ever," he said, sitting down.

The familiar, unsurprisingly, didn't answer as he hopped off to push the boat back deeper, until he was waist-deep in water, then he climbed back on with a spryness I wouldn't have expected from a man even half his age. Then, ignoring the dripping of his own clothes, the familiar walked to the wheel, turned on the motor, and sped away, leaving a large wake in his…well, wake.

Once the hum of the boat was gone, I finally exhaled. That was…something, for sure. Pinfish was wheeling and dealing with the vamp? Why hadn't he confronted the vampire about the mermaid-stunning potion? Had he thought I was lying about it? Or did he just want to overlook that where the vamp was concerned?

What else had Cal lied about? It seemed his story shifted depending on who he was speaking to. What stories had he told Big Dog? Big Jo? Maria?

I knew one thing. I needed to get to Vinnie to tell him the latest, and hopefully, he'd be able to convince the bank to give up the information about Big Jo's mortgage. Half a million dollars didn't appear and disappear, and there were only a handful of witches in town who'd have that kind of money.

It was the sort of lead I'd been waiting for. I looked at the wand and turned it over in my hand. "Well, I suppose you are good for something. Think you could transport me back to the Cove?"

The wand lay dormant in my hand, as if it had tired of my nonsense and gone to sleep.

"Come on." I shook it. "You had no problems magicking me here. Get me home."

Nothing.

"Fates alive," I muttered, turning to look at the densely packed forest all around me.

And with a scowl on my face, I began to walk.

Chapter Twenty-One

I walked for ages until I finally saw a light in the distance. It wasn't, as I'd hoped, the road so I could've called Kit or someone else to get me. Instead, it was the RV park that held the werewolf enclave. I glanced at the moon, grateful it wasn't full, and walked nervously toward the area.

I'd never actually been inside the enclave. Not that witches weren't allowed, but the wolves had always been a bit funny about their territory. Big Jo told me once that they patrolled the woods—either to hunt or keep out trespassers. It might've been smarter to turn around and head back into the swamp, but I wasn't on the worst footing with the werewolves. Someone might take pity on me and point me toward the road, at least. I walked with my hands up, knowing it was only a matter of time before one of the sharp-nosed creatures scented me.

"Who goes there?"

I froze mid-step. "It's Jo Maelstrom. Uh. The younger. Little Jo. From Witch's Cove."

The voice dripped with condescension. "Seriously? What are you doing here?"

I turned, recognizing the voice now, and gave Carver Briggs a nervous smile as he appeared from the woods, his teeth bared in a wolfish sort of way. I would've rather run into *any* other wolf, but at least he knew who I was.

"Hi, Carver. Sorry to intrude on your..." Natasha appeared beside him, and it was clear the two had been busy *patrolling* the perimeter, based on the way her top was haphazardly buttoned. "Evening. I got lost. Just looking for a way back to the road."

"How did you *get lost* here?" Carver asked, narrowing his gaze as his nostrils flared. "You stink. Have you been walking in the swamp or something?"

"You could say that," I said, hoping I might get out of this conversation without exposing the entirety of my embarrassment.

"Where's your broom?" Natasha asked, a

superior smile sliding onto her face. "Oh, that's right. You probably can't ride one, can you?"

Carver seemed emboldened by his girlfriend's cattiness and let out a chuckle. "Or did you try to ride one, and it knocked you off?"

That, at least, was a less embarrassing story than the truth. "Sure."

They shared a look of unadulterated glee.

"Anyway, I need a ride back to the Cove, if someone would be willing to help." *Not you two, obviously.* "Or you can point me in the right direction, and I'll walk—"

"Nonsense."

Big Dog's voice boomed over the three of us, and it gave *me* unadulterated glee when Carver wilted like a snow cone in July. The alpha had probably scented me, as the other two had, and now he stood on the front steps of his RV. It was, unsurprisingly, the largest and most expensive of the bunch. There also seemed to be shadows moving around inside, and I didn't want to think about what I'd interrupted him doing.

"Are you all right, Jo? You look like you've seen a ghost," Big Dog said, coming to stand beside me. He sniffed the air near my head. "And you smell like a washed-up fish. Where did you come from?"

There was the mildest hint of accusation in his voice, so I figured I'd better come clean with him or else I might find myself chewed out—literally.

"The swamp," I said.

He quirked a brow. "What were you doing there?"

I let out a sigh, wishing Carver and his too-pretty girlfriend would return to the woods to keep making out or whatever they were doing instead of staring at me.

"I cast a spell," I ground out slowly. "It went wrong."

Natasha snorted in laughter, as did Carver, but they turned their gazes to the ground when Big Dog growled.

"Dear Little Jo," Big Dog said, putting his hand on my shoulder. "Maybe you should slow down on the magic, eh? You've always had trouble with it. No use trying to fill your grandmother's shoes until you're ready."

"Yeah." I wanted to die at the patronizing tone. "I guess."

His smile was nothing but pity. "Indeed. Carver," he all but barked at his son. "Get your car, pup."

Carver jumped into action and ran into the dark, leaving Natasha, Big Dog, and me waiting awkwardly. Well, Natasha and I were standing around awkwardly, Big Dog didn't seem to have an awkward bone in his body.

"Actually, could I have a word alone with you, Big Dog?" I asked, my voice small compared to his booming one.

"Of course!" He gave Natasha one look, and she scoffed, skulking off the way Carver had gone. When the alpha turned back to me, his voice softened to normal levels. "What is it?"

"This is going to sound a little crazy," I said. "But when I said I was using the wand earlier, I was asking it to bring me something to help exonerate Aimee. Then it transported me to the swamp."

"Seems like that wand isn't doing you too many favors," he said.

"Yeah, except that I overheard a conversation between Cal Reaves and Duke Pinfish," I said.

His expression shifted. "What does that bloodsucker want with that mermaid?"

"Cal is trying to get Duke Pinfish to honor the deal he was trying to make with Maria," I said.

A low growl rumbled from the werewolf's throat. "And is the fish going for it?"

"Not yet," I said. "But there was something Pinfish said that I hadn't heard before. He said some witches had offered Maria a million dollars to sell to them instead of the vamp. Now, I know my grandmother took out a mortgage for half a million, and my hunch is that's what the money was to be used for."

"Probably a good hunch," he said.

"But what I don't know is who else contributed funds." I tilted my head in his direction. "That wasn't...you, was it?"

"No." He shook his head. "I sent Carver with our own offer."

"So this million-dollar offer only came from witches?" I asked. "If that was the case, why get involved at all?"

"I wasn't planning on it," he said. "But when your grandmother died, I assumed the deal would fall apart. After all, I heard she was the one spearheading it. I didn't want Maria to succumb to the vampire's plans, so I sent Carver to discuss another offer with her. But as we've discussed, he was unsuccessful."

It seemed to me the alpha should've teamed up *with* my grandmother to avoid that scenario prior to Big Jo's death, but something told me the alpha didn't like working with others he couldn't dominate.

"Did the vampire say what he wanted with the swamp?" Big Dog asked.

I nodded. "He wants to build a bridge from the Beach to the Hollow."

"A *bridge*? Over my lands?" The dog let out a growl that was almost feral, then a long string of filthy curses that would've made a sailor blush.

"It all hinges on Duke Pinfish now," I said. "And the only way Pinfish will sell to Cal is if I sell the Cove to the vamp. Pinfish wants it demolished."

"You aren't thinking about doing that, are you?"

he asked. "Because if you are, I'd be happy to take it off your hands."

For the first time, when I said no, I meant it. "I have no intention of selling it. The night Maria died, she was finalizing a deal to sell the land. If it wasn't the vampire, and it wasn't you, then it had to have been Big Jo's business partner," I said. "So who could that be?"

"I haven't a clue," he said. "You witches have all manner of secrets." He paused. "Surely, there's some kind of paper trail? A link to an account or something like that?"

"The bank won't tell me if there is," I said. "I'm waiting on Big Jo's death certificate to come in. Apparently, everyone knowing my name only gets me so far."

"That lawyer. Daniel. He's helping you, isn't he?"

I nodded. "He says his hands are tied too."

"Hm. We'll see about that."

Carver drove up in his very expensive car, looking chastened as he got out and opened the passenger side for me, not meeting the gaze of his alpha.

"Take her wherever she wants to go," Big Dog said. "And if I hear you saying another disparaging word about her, I'll take it out of your hide. Understand, son?"

Carver's face turned the color of a tomato. It

didn't escape my notice that Natasha seemed immune to the alpha's criticisms, as she inspected her nails off to the side.

"I'm sorry, what was that?" Big Dog barked.

"Yes, sir," Carver enunciated, his gaze still on the ground.

"Best of luck," Big Dog said to me, his face softening. "And if the police don't want to help, then you come back here, and we'll make sure to press the issue until it's resolved."

I smiled at him, feeling like I finally had someone in my corner. "Thank you. And I'm really sorry for showing up unannounced."

"Yours is always a face I don't mind seeing," he said, and based on the smile, I was sure he meant it. "But you need to be careful. Someone out there isn't above hurting people to get what they want. I would hate to see you end up like Maria."

~

Carver didn't say a word to me during the short drive, which was, in my opinion, an improvement. For a man who lived in an RV, his car was impossibly nice, all leather and an engine that more than announced its presence. And practically doused in his expensive cologne—so much so that I'd probably reek of the stuff for days. But he was giving me a ride, and I was sure I probably smelled of swamp water, so it was a fair trade.

The police station was on the edge of town,

another small, two-story place that probably held an apartment or more offices upstairs. Carver pulled his car into the empty spot in front of the station, and I got out.

"Thanks for the ride," I said.

He didn't respond, putting the car in park and turning up the radio, as if to wait for me.

I had to smile, feeling quite the spoiled witch at having a werewolf chauffeur all of a sudden, but it dropped off my face as soon as I walked through the front door.

There was one person at work at the police station, reading the latest edition of the Holl-Call. Aimee's face was plastered over it, the headline screaming that she was the cause of all the problems in the water now. I made a mental note to stop by Lewis's shop and wring his neck.

"Can I help you?" Vinnie's voice came from behind the paper.

I half-smiled. "There's been a burglary."

"Jo?" He lowered the corner of the newspaper. "What's going on? A burglary?"

"No, but I can see you're hard at work trying to clear Aimee's name," I replied.

He looked down at the paper before folding it and putting it aside. "We have proof she did it."

"A vial. Circumstantial at best."

"A vial and motive," he said, sounding a little exasperated. "What do you want?"

"I'm here to tell you that the night Maria died, she was meeting with someone to finalize a deal for the sale of her swampland near the Cove," I said. "Someone in business with my grandmother."

"Yes." The paper went back up. "Aimee."

"Aimee doesn't have access to that kind of money," I said through gritted teeth. "Someone in town was working with my grandmother to raise funds to buy the land from Maria. They'd managed to get over a million dollars. If we find who that other person is, we find Maria's killer."

"Then why not bring this to the bank?" He turned the page. "They'll probably be able to tell you who she was in business with."

"I would love to do that, but until I get her death certificate in, they aren't really talking to me," I said. "I was *hoping* the police might be able to make headway where I couldn't. Considering you're, you know, the police."

"Sorry." He pulled the paper up. "It's out of my hands now."

"What's that supposed to mean?"

"I got word from the Justice Council in New Orleans that the fishes have taken jurisdiction of this case. They've assigned their own people, have their own justice system down there. Aimee's going to be arrested any day now and taken to their place."

"And you don't care," I almost spat. "You're going to sit here and *not* do your job."

"I did my job. I investigated. Found a suspect. Handed it over to our justice department." He threw down the paper. "It's up to them to prove whether she's guilty or innocent. And if she's as *innocent* as you say, she'll be back home in no time."

I didn't trust the mermaids to be so fair to her. "Vinnie, you've got to help me out here."

"No, what I've got to do is finish reading this interesting article on the proposed new restaurant coming to Eldred's Beach," he said, pointing to the paper. "If you have a complaint, come back in the morning and tell my boss. Otherwise, beat it."

~

I was so angry I barely acknowledged Carver. He didn't say anything, except to ask where I wanted to go, and I barely managed "*Home*" before losing myself in my own furious thoughts. I'd been half joking that the police were on Cal's payroll, but based on Vinnie's response, it seemed more and more likely.

"Turn down—"

"I know where you live."

As my anger dissipated, awkwardness replaced it as I adjusted myself on the fine leather seat. It wasn't as if there were thousands of houses and people in Eldred's Hollow, and the werewolf enclave was up the road from Big Jo's property. But it still seemed weird that he knew where I lived.

He stopped at the green mailbox and gingerly

took the dirt road. His car slowed in front of the first house on the property, the log cabin, and a chill swept through me.

"Keep driving," I said.

"But this is—"

"Not my house anymore," I said, nodding toward The Shack on the other end of the property.

"You'd live there instead of a whole house?" he asked, pressing the gas.

"You wouldn't understand," I replied as the log cabin faded from view.

Carver pulled up in front of The Shack, and the whole thing creaked and moaned with excitement as I stepped out of the car.

"That place gives me the creeps," Carver said, eyeing it from the driver's seat. "You sure you want to be here?"

"Fewer ghosts here," I said, lingering on the car door. "Thanks for the ride. Appreciate it."

"What do you want me to tell Big Dog?" he asked. "Doesn't seem like you were too happy with the police. Do you need him to intervene?"

"Unless he has a way of getting me what I need from the bank, then no," I said.

"What do you need?"

"Access to Big Jo's accounts," I said. I doubted the alpha could help, but it couldn't hurt.

"I see." A pause. "I'll let him know."

Chapter Twenty-Two

"I got a call from Big Dog Briggs at seven a.m." Daniel took a long swig of his sweet tea and gave me a sideways look. "Thank you for that."

"Oh?" I replied, trying to appear innocent. "What did he say?"

"Well, apparently, he was absolutely aghast that I hadn't been working faster to get you access to your grandmother's bank records," he said, the ghost of a smirk on his face. "Namely, some kind of joint account she'd set up."

"And what did you tell him?"

"That I was working on it." He pulled out an

envelope from his pocket. "And this arrived late yesterday. Guess the lawyer route was quicker than the family route this time."

I stared at the envelope for a moment before grabbing it out of his hands, tearing it open and pulling out the paper inside. The death certificate.

"Heart attack, as we suspected," Daniel said, pointing to the line.

I stared at it, the cause of death looking back at me as if it were the morning's weather. Crazy how a whole life could be summed up in two words. *Myocardial infarction.* With all the magic she had, Big Jo hadn't been able to avoid such a simple and common death.

Suddenly, I was back on the front porch of the cabin, listening to the police officer as he told me how my parents' car had...

"Jo?"

I looked up, remembering I was sitting at the cafe. "Yes?"

There was concern in his blue eyes. Blue? Had he always had blue eyes? "Are you all right?"

"Fine." I quickly folded the paper and put it in my back pocket, swallowing the lump in my throat. "What's my next move?"

"Have you found the will yet?" Daniel asked.

"No."

"Well, that would be the best thing, but maybe with the death certificate, the ladies at the bank will be more amenable to helping you out," Daniel said. "And if they won't, then they'd better gird their loins because Big Dog seems out for blood." He cast me another sideways glance. "Any idea what that's about?"

"Don't really feel like sharing that with you," I said.

He made a face. "Why not?"

"Because it'll probably end up on the front page of the Holl-Call," I said. "Bad enough Lewis has it in for Aimee. Don't want to add fuel to the fire."

"Lewis?" He rubbed the back of his neck. "I don't talk with Lewis about my clients, Jo. In fact, we don't even talk business."

"Then what do you talk about?"

"Sailing," he said. "I've got a Hobie catamaran. He lives on a 30-foot sailboat over in the bay."

I shook my head. "What?"

"We also both like history. He got me onto this podcast about the magical side of the Civil War," he said, his face a little lighter. "There's also the usual camaraderie of being a pair of transplants to Eldred's Hollow."

"You aren't a transplant," I said with a scoff. "You grew up here."

"I *summered* here. As did Lewis. There's a difference." He smiled at me. "Did you really think I was sharing all your secrets with him? I'm a professional, Jo."

It was hard to believe that with his wrinkled button-up shirt, old boating shoes, and holey jeans. But the look in his eyes was sincere, and some of my anger evaporated.

"I still think he's a slimy little weasel," I said. "And I question your judgment."

"Fair." He cracked a wry smile. "If you want to talk with my questionable judgment in private, though, my office is open."

That sounded nice, actually, but unfortunately, I had pressing matters to attend to. "I'll be sure to tell you once I figure everything out. But in the meantime, I have to get to the bank." I tossed down a twenty. "Paying you back for the other day."

"You don't have to—"

"It's done," I said. "Thanks, Kit!"

My friend gave me a bewildered wave before I walked out the door.

I held my breath as Sherry looked over the certificate. I prayed to the Fates that it would be enough, because I didn't know what I'd do if it wasn't. Even with all Big Dog's bluster and bravado, I doubted he'd be any match for these meek, rule-following witches.

"Ideally, we'd like to have some formal proof that you're her next of kin," Sherry said, folding the paper up and handing it back to me.

I had to swallow my biting remark.

"But I suppose we can make an exception now."

"You can make an exception now?" I lifted a brow. "Why not before?"

"To be honest, there was some...*concern* about the cause of Big Jo's death," she said. "She'd made some large transactions in the months preceding it. In these situations, it's always best to err on the side of caution." She tilted her head. "Especially in light of poor Maria's death, too. This amount of money can make people do some crazy things."

"I didn't..." I cleared my throat. "Anyway. Now that's all cleared up, can you *please* tell me about this mortgage and where the money went?"

"Of course, give me one moment." She turned to her computer and began typing. After a minute, she turned her monitor around to show me. "Three months ago, Jo Maelstrom, your grandmother, of course, took out a mortgage against her homestead property and Witch's Cove for $500,000. She then wired that money to..." She pulled the screen back around, typing and waiting again, then turned it back to me. "An account started under the name Witch's Cove, LLC." Screen back toward her. More typing. "There were a few other deposits in that account, totaling over one million doll—" She stopped. "Hm..." She typed, concern falling over her face. "Well, this is odd."

"What is it?"

"It seems the account is zeroed out." She turned

the monitor back to me for a brief moment. "Yes, this is quite odd. I'm sure it's a glitch or something. I'd checked it the other day when you came to see us and there was a million in there." She typed again and bit her lip. "I'm so sorry, Jo. It looks like the other owner on the account came in to take the money."

"And who was that?" I asked, leaning forward.

"Let me see." More typing. More waiting. "Ah, yes. Looks like the owners of the account are Jo Maelstrom and…Stuart Eaves."

The ferry pulled into the dock, and nerves skittered down my arms. I had Big Jo's wand stashed in its usual place. There were plenty of people waiting to board, which made me feel a little braver. I wasn't about to approach a potential murderer by myself, but I owed it to Stuart to talk with him before I went to the police. There was still some small part of me that hoped it was all one big misunderstanding.

The ferry docked, and Stuart was there, bidding farewell to the departing witches and hello to the ones climbing on board. I held my breath and walked up, hoping my unease wasn't plain on my face.

"Hey there, Little Jo!" He waved. "Off to the beach again?"

"Yeah," I said with a curt nod, passing by to find

a spot on the deck. My plan was to wait until we were underway, then approach him on the bridge. He couldn't quite get away from me there, and we'd have to hash it out over the hour it would take to get to the other side.

The ferry left the dock, the waters much calmer than the last time I'd taken this trip, and I checked my phone absentmindedly for the millionth time. After ten minutes, I rose stiffly and walked up the stairs.

Stuart was on the bridge by himself, steering the boat. He turned when the door opened and his face brightened.

"Oh, hello. Come to try to steer the ship again?" He chuckled. "Remember when you used to do that?"

Vaguely. I'd probably been ten years old. The thought made what I was going to confront him about that much more upsetting. "I actually had something I wanted to ask you about," I said, my pulse quickening.

"Shoot."

"I finally got access to Big Jo's accounts," I said. "She'd transferred a large sum of money into an account held jointly by the two of you."

I couldn't see his expression, but a ripple crossed his shoulders. "Yeah? We were going into business together."

"Are you the one Maria met with on the night

of her death?" I asked. "The one who was going to offer her a million dollars not to sell to Cal Reaves. The one who..." I swallowed. "The one who doused her with stunning potion before leaving her to die?"

He turned, and before I could react, he had his wand in his hand, flinging a spell in my direction and sending me backward toward the wall, pinning my hands magically behind my back.

"What the—Stuart!" I gasped, struggling to reach for Big Jo's wand. But it wriggled its way free from my hiding spot and floated over to Stuart, who snatched it out of the air.

"I'll take this," he said, tucking it into his pocket. "Not as if it's any use to you, but apparently you've had flashes of brilliance lately, and I don't want to take that risk."

I couldn't believe what was happening. I'd grown up with Stuart. He'd been a dear friend of my grandmother, and now...now he was stealing money and killing mermaids?

"Why?" It was the only word that came to mind.

"All you had to do was sell to Cal." Stuart shook his head. "It seemed like a sure thing. You'd walk away with a huge chunk of change, the vamp could bulldoze the bar. Then everyone could've had their happily ever after."

"Except the citizens of Witch's Cove," I said. "This had nothing to do with the bridge, did it?"

"No. He can build it. Or not build it."

I shifted with a start. "Maria knew you'd drained the accounts, didn't she? She was going to tell people you stole Big Jo's money, wasn't she? *That's* why you killed her."

"She came to me that night, said she still wanted to be in business. That she was getting tired of fending off Cal's proposals, and didn't want to sell to the werewolves, so she wanted to close the deal. But I told her I wasn't interested in moving forward without Big Jo. I'd hoped she'd leave it alone, but she persisted. Asked me what I was going to do with Big Jo's money, and when I didn't answer, she figured out my plan."

"Good for her," I said, even though she'd ended up dead because of it.

"She said it wasn't right. I told her the writing was on the wall, and she should take Cal's money. He was gonna buy up every other piece of land and get his way. No use standing in the way of progress, especially if there was money to be made. She didn't take too kindly to that."

"I'm sure she didn't."

"She said she was going to meet with Lewis and reveal what I'd done. Told me it was going to be on the front page of the Holl-Call, and I'd have the police knocking on my door."

That's why she had his card the night she died. "So you doused her with mermaid-stunning potion," I said. "And left her to die."

He didn't look at me. I hoped he was wracked with guilt, at least.

"How could you let Aimee take the blame?" That wasn't worse than actual *murder*, but it was still horrible.

"I confess, I was panicking a little after it happened," he said. "Came to the Cove so I'd have an alibi. I heard you two arguing in the office. Thought it might be a good place to hide the vial. After all, Aimee's known for—"

"Yes, yes, we all know," I snapped, fury rising in me once more. "None of this was necessary, Stuart."

"Except it was." He turned to me. "This boat is costing me more to keep it afloat than it makes. With the money, I can retire and live somewhere nice."

"It's only a million," I said with a look. "If you're going to murder someone, might as well do it for two or three."

"Well, beggars can't be choosers." He turned back to me, his wand back in his hand. "I've got to get this boat to the dock and disembark my passengers. Then you and I are going to take a little detour."

Before I could answer, an invisible force pulled me upright and backward until I stumbled into a very cramped room with life jackets, buoys, and an anchor that smelled of salt water. The only light was a small porthole.

"Why don't you hang out here for a bit?" He started to shut the door before pausing. "And don't even try calling for help. I've soundproofed it."

"Someone's going to notice I'm missing," I said, kicking myself for not telling Daniel or Kit or *someone* where I was going.

"They'll probably assume you went back to your old life," he said, leaning on the doorframe. "I'll make sure that fancy rental car gets back to its home, don't you worry."

And with that, he shut the door.

Not that I'd ever been cuffed or bound, but the magical bindings seemed much more uncomfortable than their non-magical counterparts. I couldn't stand—could barely get my feet under me before the magic pulled me back down. There was an anchor point sticking into my thigh, and my shoulders hurt from the awkward angle. But that paled in comparison to my anger at Stuart's betrayal. Not just me, but my grandmother, Maria, Aimee. Everyone in Eldred's Hollow. He was the literal definition of take the money and run.

Sometime after Stuart locked me in here, the swaying of the boat slowed, and my pulse quickened. We'd docked, and if I had to guess, Stuart was telling the prospective customers on the other side that he was taking the boat in for maintenance or something. Where was he going to take me?

The Gulf, probably. Somewhere he could shove me overboard, and nobody would find me.

There was a shadow outside the window, and I furrowed my brow. It floated by the window again, and I caught a flash of white features.

"Jimbo?" I called, even though my voice wouldn't carry beyond this room. "Jimbo, is that you?"

The seagull latched on to the porthole edge, wings flapping as he struggled to hold on. *"Ha-ha-haaaa!"*

"Jimbo," I called. "Go get help. Daniel, or Kit, or someone. Aimee, even. Tell them where I am!"

"*Ha-ha-haaaa!*"

I swear, if that birdbrain was looking for a french fry at a time like this...

"Please," I said, a little desperation crawling into my voice. "Get someone to help me! Stuart's the one who killed Maria, and he's going to do the same to me!"

The engine of the boat rumbled abruptly, and Jimbo's grip on the porthole loosened. He disappeared for a moment before flapping his wings and rising back up. He let out one loud *ha-ha-haaaa* before flying away.

My only hope of being saved lay with a seagull.

"Fates alive," I muttered, trying to get up again. But for all my effort, I remained stubbornly where I was, and finally, with a sigh, I gave up and resigned myself to sit there until Stuart came for me.

When the door opened, my heart jumped into my throat. Stuart looked gray-faced and angry, as if it were *my* fault he was having to do this. He reached into the closet and pulled me out, releasing the magical hold on me. I fought, but he'd cast some kind of charm to give his old body more strength. That, or I was weak.

"Stuart, I—"

The next thing I knew, I was falling backward, my back hitting the water with a stinging splash. I sank, the magical bonds still holding my hand together, unable to swim toward the surface, as the sun moved farther and farther away.

Until suddenly, I stopped sinking. Rough hands gripped my arms and I found myself staring into a familiar face.

"Duke Pinfish?" I attempted to say, but my words were only bubbles.

Great.

But instead of taking me to his underwater lair, he pushed me up, overpowering Stuart's charms and helping me to the surface. But we didn't stop there —the water funneled around us, pushing me higher until he set me gently on the deck of the ferry.

"D-Duke Pinfish?" I said as soon as I could breathe. "How did you, what did you—"

Jimbo fluttered down to perch happily on his

shoulder, looking quite proud of himself.

"Your familiar came squawking to me," Pinfish said. "Told me you'd found Maria's killer and were yourself in danger. He's quite loyal, this one."

I wasn't sure what surprised me more—that Pinfish could understand Jimbo's squawks or that the seagull had *actually* gone to find help instead of stalking a drive-through.

"T-thank you," I said, shakily before I came back to myself. "Stuart killed Maria. He and my grandmother were trying to buy the land off Maria to keep the vampire away. After Big Jo died, Stuart thought he'd keep all the money for himself. Maria was going to go to the press about it." I exhaled, scarcely able to believe I'd lived to tell the tale.

But I had, as two mermaids had Stuart by the arms, with their spears pressed against him. He looked white as a sheet as he babbled about them having the wrong person.

"Take him to the council," Pinfish said. "I'm sure he'll have a lot to say to our magistrate."

Jimbo let out a loud *ha-ha* and took flight off the mermaid's shoulder, pecking at Stuart.

"You confounded vermin!" Stuart barked. "Get away from me!"

But Jimbo found what he was looking for, pulling Big Jo's wand from Stuart's back pocket and flapping back over to drop it in my hands. He settled on my shoulder, and I reached up to put a shaky hand on his head.

"T-thanks," I said.

"Now, you can take him," Pinfish said with a nod.

The two mermaids slapped a bubble-looking thing over Stuart's mouth then dove into the murky depths with him. Within seconds, the water stilled.

"Yikes," I said.

"I suppose I owe you a debt for discovering Maria's killer," Pinfish said, surveying me. "You have your grandmother's tenacity, for sure."

"You are going to leave Aimee alone, right?" I said.

"As long as I never see that abhorrent potion on her person again," he said, before disappearing into the waves.

I was alone on the ferry now, without a *clue* how to drive or steer it. Jimbo landed on my shoulder, clipping his beak toward the wand still in my hand.

"I don't know, buddy," I said. "It's pretty temperamental."

Ha-ha-ha.

"All right, we'll give it a try." I held my breath. "Get me home?"

Magic rushed through me, and the rocking of the boat stilled.

"Jo?"

I opened my eyes. Aimee was behind the bar. Somehow, someway, I'd managed to get myself back home.

"Give me a Witchwhacker," I said, stumbling toward the bar. "We have a *lot* to talk about."

Chapter Twenty-Three

By the next morning, the story of Stuart's betrayal and subsequent aquatic arrest was the talk of the town. No one knew the whole story, of course, and it had given me the greatest pleasure to tell Lewis to talk with my seagull familiar if he wanted to know exactly what had happened. I was too grateful that the mermaids were no longer at war with us to ask Pinfish how he'd managed to communicate with Jimbo.

All charges against Aimee were dropped immediately, too. Vinnie didn't seem too thrilled that a hapless witch had done his job better than he had, but I tried to be graceful in my victory.

Unfortunately, Daniel said it would take weeks, perhaps even years, before we got Stuart back and could even begin to reclaim the money he'd stolen. While the mermaids had been given the all-clear to return to the Cove and spend their money, it still meant we were barely making ends meet.

"You should rent the property out then," Daniel said, as I ate my weight in grits, eggs, and biscuits that morning, the sheer relief of having solved the mystery unlocking my appetite. Kit was pleased, of course, and kept bringing me more food as soon as my plate was empty.

"Rent out the property?" I frowned. "I'm not letting that blood-sucking vampire—"

"Not to him," Daniel said. "To someone who needs a place to live. You could rent The Shack and the cabin out for a good price, and that should be enough to cover your note for the mortgage." He paused. "You are planning on going back to Atlanta, aren't you?"

"I am, but…"

"But?" Kit stopped, a plate of pancakes floating behind her.

"But I'm coming back," I said, ducking my head to hide a smile. "Fates know Aimee needs help, and there's still a lot to untangle here. I'm not leaving her with a mess to deal with by herself, and—"

"Mm-hm," Kit said with a knowing smile. "Sure

thing, Jo."

"What about your job?" Daniel asked.

"I need to repair things with my boss a bit, but when we talked yesterday, he said he doesn't want to lose me," I said. "So we're going to do a trial run of me working remotely and traveling back and forth. I can't say it'll be a permanent solution, but at least until we figure everything out." I put my head on my hands. "And an extra paycheck would certainly help make ends meet."

"Then at least rent out the cabin," Daniel said. "It's got several bedrooms, right? I'm sure someone's looking for a place."

"As it so happens," Kit said, giving me a sideways look, "I'm actually looking for a place. Not that I don't *love* living with my parents but..." She leaned across the counter. "Living *and* working for them? Not my favorite."

"I heard that, Kitty."

She winced and kept walking with the pancakes.

"I don't know if I can rent out the cabin," I said to Daniel. "I haven't set foot in there since my parents died. I doubt Big Jo had, either. It's too..." I shivered. "It's too much."

"Then ask for help," he said. "I'll come. I'm sure Kit will, too. Aimee surely owes you several thousand favors. The whole of the Cove would probably be happy to—"

"No." I shook my head. "No, I need to... You

and Kit are fine. Aimee, too. It's hard to explain—"

"You don't have to," Daniel said, throwing down a fifty. "Got yours today."

"This seems to be a recurring theme," I said. "I pay, you pay. It's almost like a—" I stopped myself before I said "date" because it certainly wasn't that. "Thank you. And thank you for all your help."

"Well, next time a warlock has you tied up in a boat, be sure to send your seagull my way," he said, walking toward the back. "Be happy to come rescue you."

"Mm-hmm, I bet he would," Kit said, walking by with a carafe of coffee.

"Hush."

Before I left, Kit reiterated that she would very much like to rent the cabin from me, but understood if that was too much to bear. Still, I couldn't help but see the utility of the solution. It was putting into service an asset I owned free and clear. The only requirement was for me to face my fears.

I stood on the front porch for at least half an hour, unable to take a step forward. What might I find in there? A house, completely the same as it had been eight years ago? Was there still food in the fridge? What about my bedroom, was it—

"You won't know until you open the door, Jo," I muttered to myself, walking forward and putting my hand on the knob.

It turned for me—good ol' familiarity charms—and the door swung open.

I exhaled loudly.

There wasn't… Everything was gone. The couches, the artwork, even the chairs under the island. But in the center of the living room was a single stool with an envelope addressed to me in Big Jo's handwriting.

Dear Jo,

I hope I'm writing this letter years before it's ever read. But I have a feeling my time here on this plane is coming to an end sooner than I'd like, and since you aren't answering my phone calls, I thought a letter would suffice. I only hope you don't spend weeks dithering and avoiding the cabin before you find it.

I cleared my throat. Even in death, Big Jo was trying to get me to be more than I was.

I wanted to give you insight into some things that are happening. I've kept them close to the vest because I'm not sure who I can trust in town—and you know how people talk here. The first is that Cal Reaves intends to destroy Eldred's Hollow. He's buying up farmland like it's going out of style, and he's offered me more and more money for this land and the Cove. I've told him to take a hike every time, of course. No amount of money would get me to sell my beloved bar.

I got wind that he was pressuring Maria Greenfin—you'll remember her as a mermaid who spent time on the shore, but now she's the leader of the sound mermaids. She controls a spit of swampland due east of the Cove, and I have it on good authority that Cal wants to buy it to build a bridge between the Beach and the interstate, and it would run right through the Hollow. We can't let him do this. Our town would cease to exist and everyone in it would scatter.

To that end, Stuart and I have started a consortium of witches to gather funds to buy it from Maria. Right now it's just the two of us, but I'd always hoped there would be more. Stuart, of course, would lose his livelihood if this bridge were built, and I know plenty of other witches would rather get burned than see our beloved town turned into another one of Cal Reaves's strip malls. The money has been pooled into an account at First Hollow Bank on Main Street, under a false name, of course. The last thing we want is for word to get out and the vampire to undercut our deal.

I know you've moved on, and Eldred's Hollow isn't in your life plans anymore. But I want you to know that even though you don't think so, you belong here. I plan to leave the Cove and everything to you, and I hope you'll consider keeping it and coming home for good. Selfishly, I hope that it isn't my untimely passing that brings you here, though.

Enclosed, you'll find my will and ingredients for the Witchwhacker machine. The latter is a closely guarded secret, so don't be sharing it with any long-toothed individuals who'll try to replicate it and sell it at a fancy bar. The former, I hope, will help with solving any issues with my estate.

You are, and have always been, my favorite granddaughter. My only wish is that I could've seen you grow into the witch you're destined to become.

All my love,
Big Jo

PS: Over the summer, I finally got around to cleaning everything out. I know you don't love The Shack, so if you ever decide you'd like to move back home, this place is ready for you.

I wiped away tears, knowing if I let them continue, I'd dissolve into a puddle on the floor. I folded up the letter and tucked it into my jeans, taking extra care with the Witchwhacker recipe and the will. Daniel had started in motion the process to formally put all the property in my name, and this would only help solidify things.

I left the cabin, texting Kit that the place was all ready for her to move in whenever she wanted, and getting a string of exclamation marks in return, and walked the length of the property back toward The Shack. It swung open the front door to greet me, but as I walked inside, the couch was gone.

"Where's my bed?" I said, a little warning in my voice.

It rustled a curtain, and when I peered through the window, the couch was sitting in the field.

"Very funny," I said.

The sliding glass door opened, and outside, the rickety stairs slapped against the risers.

I followed the request, walking up until I reached the top floor, and I could've fallen over from shock.

It was completely different. And...familiar? A new bed, but somehow...my bed from my home in Atlanta sat in the center of the room. Artwork plucked from my walls, too. The bedside tables, the lamps, the clothes in the closet. All mine.

"I'm going to assume it was a charm," I said, eyeing the house warily. "A charm set to begin when I said I was moving home. Not that you're a powerful enough house to literally summon my things from five hundred miles away."

The curtains rustled.

"Mm-hm." I turned on my heel, before stopping and smiling. "Thank you. This all looks lovely."

The planks of the deck rattled.

"Where do you think I'm going?" I said with a shake of my head.

Aimee was taking a well-deserved day off, so it was up to me to open the bar. The wand worked perfectly, rolling up the windows, starting the Witchwhacker machine, getting all the chairs off the bar. All our monthly renters had returned too, so I took my time chatting with them. Every one said they'd be happy to pay the full month, except Billy, who seemed furious that I was on good terms with the merfolk again.

Just before we opened the bar, a large, white truck pulled up, followed by an expensive black car. Cal Reaves stepped out, Dietrich emerged from the truck, and before long, the familiar was pushing a large white fridge toward the Cove.

"What's this?" I asked, keeping my distance in case they meant to stuff me in it.

"I've come to deliver the blood you asked for," Cal said, sauntering into the bar as if he owned it.

"Thank you," I said with a thin smile. I'd forgotten all about that. "I'm sure that'll come in handy."

"Such a horrible turn of events," he drawled, sitting down at the bar. "Stuart Eaves was such a nice fellow. Wonder what made him turn so..." He gestured in the air. "Hateful?"

"Money makes people do crazy things," I said, picking up a rag and wiping down the bar.

"So I hear you're staying," he said. "What about that nice job in Atlanta?"

"Allowing me to work remotely," I said. "At least for the moment."

"Remotely." He shook his head. "This world is moving too fast for me sometimes."

"Seems like I'm here for the long haul," I said, hoping he was getting my meaning without me having to spell it out. "Which probably means your deal with Duke Pinfish is off."

He gave me a sideways look. "Whatever do you mean?"

I could've kicked myself. I'd been privy to that conversation accidentally. "Just that…well, you were still trying to get that land from Pinfish, right?"

"As I told you, I can't comment on pending negotiations," he said. The twitch in his mouth told me Pinfish had declined his offer. "But you know, I'm a very patient man. I eventually get what I want, even if it takes a few hundred years."

"Well, best of luck to you." I put both hands on the bar, sending a message. "Because this bar's going to be in Maelstrom hands for a while yet."

He smiled, showing off his fangs. "Enjoy the blood, Ms. Maelstrom. I'm sure I'll be seeing much more of you in the coming months."

Acknowlegments

This book was a lovely little break in the middle of writing my cozy fantasy series, The Weary Dragon Inn. If you haven't noticed, I borrowed a lot from real life places, many inhabited by my husband in his youth. The Shack, the log cabin, even the Cove are all based on real places in Elberta, Alabama. You should absolutely visit sometime.

Of course, my thanks first and foremost go to my husband, who continues to be my most ardent supporter and who patiently walked me through the legal process of probate in Alabama. If anyone has any quibbles with the legal advice given in this book, take it up with him.

Thanks also to my village of grandparents and great aunts who love my kids and, more importantly, love hanging out with my kids, so I can get work done. Special kudos to the NaNoWriMo friends who sprinted with me in November of 2023.

As always, Chelsea, my beta reader, Danielle, my amazing editor, Lisa, my QA check—appreciate all of you.

Also By the Author

The Weary Dragon Inn Series

Bev may not know who she was before she showed up in the quaint village of Pigsend five years ago, but that doesn't bother her much. She's made a tidy little life for herself as the proprietor of the Weary Dragon Inn, where the most notable event is when she makes her famous rosemary bread. But when earthquakes and sinkholes start appearing all over town, including near Bev's front door, she's got to put on her sleuthing hat to figure out what—or who—might be causing them before the entire town disappears.

Drinks and Sinkholes is the first book in the Weary Dragon Inn series, and is available in ebook, physical, and audiobook at your favorite retailer.

Also By the Author

Lexie Carrigan Chronicles

Lexie Carrigan thought she was weird enough until her family drops a bomb on her—she's magical. Now the girl who's never made waves is blowing up her nightstand and no one seems to want to help her. That is, until a kind gentleman shows up with all the answers. But Lexie finds out being magical is the least weird thing about her.

Spells and Sorcery is the first book in the Lexie Carrigan Chronicles, and is available now in eBook, physical, and audiobook at your favorite retailer.

About the Author

S. Usher Evans was born and raised in Pensacola, Florida. After a decade of fighting bureaucratic battles as an IT consultant in Washington, DC, she suffered a massive quarter-life-crisis. She found fighting dragons was more fun than writing policy, so she moved back to Pensacola to write books full-time. She currently resides there with her husband and kids, and frequently can be found plotting on the beach.

For a full list of titles by S. Usher Evans, visit her website http://www.susherevans.com/